Claudia and the Perfect Boy

Claudia and the Perfect Boy

Ann M. Martin

AN
APPLE
PAPERBACK

SCHOLASTIC INC.
New York Toronto London Auckland Sydney

Cover art by Hodges Soileau

ISBN 0-590-47009-4

12 11 10 9 8 7 6 5 4 3 2 1   4 5 6 7 8/9

Printed in the U.S.A.   40

First Scholastic printing, January 1994

The author gratefully acknowledges
Suzanne Weyn
for her help in
preparing this manuscript.

Claudia and the Perfect Boy

CHAPTER 1

I would have died if anyone had seen what I was doing! I mean, it was *so* embarrassing.

But, embarrassing or not, there I was sitting at the end of my bed, hugging myself. Why? Because I wanted to know how it would feel to be locked in a dreamy, romantic embrace with the boy of my dreams.

It was seeing Logan and Mary Anne together that made me think about it. That afternoon when I was walking home from school with my friend Mary Anne Spier and her steady boyfriend, Logan Bruno, they seemed so happy. You can tell they are really crazy about each other. One minute they're laughing, teasing, and using all their little private code names and jokes. The next, their heads are together, all serious, as if they're talking about something special that's just between the two of them. (Sigh.) Mary Anne is so lucky to feel that way about a boy who feels the same way about her.

Logan and Mary Anne walked me as far as my house on Bradford Court. I stood on my front steps for a minute before going in, and I watched them as they playfully bumped into one another on their way down the street.

After that, I went straight upstairs and began hugging myself.

Who was this boy of my dreams I was pretending to hug? Good question. I hadn't met him yet. I've gone out on dates, but it's never been anything serious. That super-special, tingly, in-love thing has never happened to me. (By the way, "me" is Claudia. Claudia Kishi.)

Well, I'd thought I'd had the in-love feeling before. When I went on a vacation to California, I met a boy I really liked a lot. And before that I'd liked a couple of other boys. But nothing has come of any of it. I mean, none of those boys ever became my steady boyfriend or anything like that. And I wasn't particularly missing or thinking about those boys, either. So I probably hadn't been feeling the *real*, true in-love feeling.

Still, I remembered how nice spending time with Terry in California had been. And seeing Mary Anne and Logan together that afternoon really made me want a steady boyfriend of my own. I wasn't about to settle for just anybody, though. I wanted the perfect boy, one who was everything I dreamed of. I believed he was out there, too. He had to be.

I stretched out on my bed (hugging yourself gets boring very fast) and lay there wondering what my perfect boy would look like. I didn't care if he was Japanese-American, like I am. He would have to be cute, though. And tall. At least taller than me, and I'm about medium height for my age (which is thirteen).

Besides basic cuteness and tallness, I didn't have any specific looks requirements. Except muscles. He did have to have some muscles. But not too many muscles. I don't like those big weight-lifter muscles but I don't like skinny arms on a guy, either. Something right in the middle would be fine.

Trying to picture this perfect guy made me wonder what exactly I was looking for. After all, if you weren't sure what you wanted, you might not recognize it when you found it. It would be sort of tragic if Mr. Perfect walked right by me and I didn't even realize it.

That's when I decided I better make a list. A list of all the important qualities I was looking for in Mr. Perfect.

Bending upside down, with one hand holding my long black hair up so it wouldn't touch the floor, I searched under my bed for a pad of paper which I remembered had gotten kicked under there. (Although my room is on the messy side, I usually have a very good idea of where everything is.)

Here's what I came back up with: a bag of Cool Ranch Doritos; the Nancy Drew book I was reading; and a box of stationery with a red, green, and gold Mexican print border. I couldn't reach the pad, but that was all right. The Mexican print stationery would do. I was glad to have found these things.

I ripped open the Doritos. I'm just wild about junk food. It's stashed all over my room. I hide it because my parents don't approve of my eating junk food. Technically, I suppose they're right. Junk food is not healthy. But I'm slim and I have good skin — so what's the harm?

As I munched away, I flipped open the Nancy Drew book to the place where I'd left off reading the night before. Just like my junk food, I also have to keep my collection of Nancy Drew books hidden because they're another thing my parents disapprove of. They don't think Nancy Drew mysteries are *intellectual* enough. I don't understand how they can say that, though. You use your brain plenty when you read a mystery. After all, throughout the book you're trying to figure out who committed the crime. A good mystery is totally brain-engaging. But Mom and Dad want me to be a scholar like my sixteen-year-old sister, Janine.

Janine is a true-to-life genius who already takes college classes. That's fine for Janine, but not for me. School just isn't that interesting to me. I do enough school work to get by, but academics is *not* my strong point.

Anyway, looking down at my Nancy Drew book reminded me of Nancy's steady boyfriend, Ned Nickerson. Now Ned is a nearly perfect guy. He's athletic, smart, nice, and totally devoted to Nancy. He's always there for her, but he doesn't get in her way or try to boss her around. He lets Nancy be her own person. Nancy and Ned have a very independent relationship.

Maybe it was too independent. It worked for Nancy since she was always off solving crimes, but I wanted a guy who was around a bit more often than Ned. Come to think of it, Ned didn't have much sense of humor, either. I was definitely looking for someone who could make me laugh. That was *very* important.

I put the book aside and took out a piece of stationery. It was time for my list. I started with what I already knew.

Handsome
mussels (not too many, not to few)
Taller then me
Funny (extreamly)

Chewing the eraser of my pencil, I stopped to think about what else I expected of Mr. Perfect. A few more things came to mind right away, so I wrote them down.

Atheletic
Sensative
Easy to talk to (a good lisner)
Intresting (lots to say)

Did I want him to be artistic, like me? I *love* art of any kind and I'm pretty good at it. (I'm not being conceited, it's just true.) Pottery, sculpture, drawing, painting, print-making — you name it — I love to do anything artistic.

My perfect guy would have to appreciate art and it would be even better if he was a good artist himself. (I closed my eyes and envisioned the two of us in an artists' studio painting side by side. Heaven!) I began writing again.

Artistic
Good dreser

After a moment's thought, I almost crossed out *good dresser* since it sounded a little shallow. Was it really important?

Maybe it wouldn't be to another person, but we were talking about *my* Mr. Perfect and fashion is important to me. I think it's linked to my love of art. The way I dress is an expression of who I am, and who I am is artistic. I don't like to look like everyone else around me because I'm not like everyone else around me. So I put things together the way *I* like. For instance, that could mean wearing clay jewelry I've made myself and matching it with a belt I've added clay pieces to. I also like to experiment with the way colors look and I combine them in ways that please me. (You'd be amazed by the colors that go together. Take pink and gold. You might not think to wear pink socks with gold stretch pants, and then add a gold turtleneck under a pink sweater. But that's what I did yesterday, and then I added blue jewelry. It was great! I looked like a human sunset. The outfit made me very happy.)

No, there was no way I could see myself with a slobby dresser. That was out. He had to have some sense of fashion. *Good dresser* stayed on the list.

What else was important to me? It would be nice if Mr. Perfect was a good speller, since I can't spell for anything. In my opinion, words should be spelled the way they sound. For example, the word *enough* should be spelled *enuf*. The way it's really spelled makes it look as if it should be pronounced *ee-now-guh*. I don't know who decided how words should be spelled but I think that person went out of his or her way to be difficult. But, if Mr. Perfect were around to correct my spelling, it would be a big help. So, I made another addition to my list.

Good spellar (willing to corect mine)

That worried me, though. I didn't want him correcting *everything* I did, just my spelling. Being criticized all the time would be horrible. So I made another addition to my list.

not criticul

Then I added the most important thing about Mr. Perfect.

Crazey about me

He had to think I was great. It would be fair because I would think the same of him. (Of course I would, since he'd be perfect.) That was the part which would make everything so wonderful. I'd be loved by a boy who was perfect for me.

At that moment, my best friend, Stacey McGill, appeared at my bedroom door. "Hi," she said, tossing a flowered overnight bag onto my bed. She was planning to stay over at my house that night since it was Friday and we didn't have school the next day.

"What are you doing?" she asked, eyeing my paper.

Feeling a little embarrassed, I shoved the paper back in the stationery box. "Nothing. Just writing some thoughts, that's all."

Stacey's eyes narrowed suspiciously. "You? Writing? And no one is forcing you to do it?"

I understood her confusion. I'm not much for writing. I'd rather express myself with a picture or even a sculpture. "Well, you know," I said. "I was just trying to work out some things I've been thinking about. I wanted to see how they'd look written down."

"Anything in particular?" she asked, brushing a strand of her permed, blonde hair off her face.

"No, just some stuff."

Stacey glanced at the digital clock on my desk. "I hope you don't mind my getting here before the meeting," she said. "I just thought we could hang out."

"Sure," I replied. The meeting she was talking about was a meeting of our baby-sitting business, The Baby-sitters Club. We members call it the BSC, for short.

Besides art and fashion, the BSC is the other most important thing in my life. I really like taking care of the kids I sit for. I like earning money, too. (Between buying junk food treats, Nancy Drew books, and art supplies, money just flies out of my hands. It's a good thing I have a way to earn more.) But, for me, the most important thing about the BSC is the people in it. We are very close. Stacey may be my *best* friend, but I love all the members of the club.

Let me tell you about them. . . .

CHAPTER 2

By five-thirty that day my room was filled with laughter and happily chatting voices. "Okay, everybody," Kristy Thomas said over the noise. She shifted in my director's chair (her usual spot) and took her pencil out from over her ear. "This meeting of the Baby-sitters Club is about to start."

That's all it took to quiet everybody down. Kristy is the president of the BSC and everyone respects (and likes) her a lot. The club was her idea in the first place. She thought of it one day when her mom was making a million phone calls trying to find a sitter for Kristy's little brother, David Michael. It occurred to Kristy that it would be a great idea if her mother could call one number and reach a whole bunch of sitters at one time. That was the beginning of Kristy's simple, but brilliant, money-making brainstorm — to form the Baby-sitters Club.

She told her idea to Mary Anne (who is Kristy's best friend) and they told me. Luckily, I have my own phone and my own phone number. That's why the meetings are held in my room. Parents can call here without tying up anyone's family phone.

We worried that three members might not be enough for a club. I suggested Stacey, whom I'd met not long before. (She'd just moved to Stoneybrook.) Stacey joined and we began our new business.

Stacey, Kristy, Mary Anne, and I put up fliers around town and placed an ad in the paper telling parents to call my number every Monday, Wednesday, and Friday from five-thirty to six if they wanted to reach four reliable sitters.

Talk about instant success! We got so many calls that our four-sitter version of the BSC didn't last long. We needed another sitter as soon as parents started telling each other about our great service. We had more business than we could handle. Luckily, Mary Anne had just met Dawn Schafer. She was new to Stoneybrook, but Mary Anne had gotten to know her pretty well. We asked Dawn to become a BSC member and she joined.

At that point everything was pretty much under control and calm. But with us, nothing seems to stay calm for long. Because then Stacey had to move away. (I'll tell you why later.) While Stacey was gone, we took on two junior members, Jessi Ramsey and Mallory (Mal) Pike, to fill in for Stacey. (They're called *junior* because they're eleven and can only sit in the daytime.) Then Stacey returned (hurray!) and the BSC was up to seven members.

By then our business was *booming*. We were so busy that we took on two associate members — Logan, and a friend of Kristy's named Shannon Kilbourne. They don't usually attend meetings, but we call them if we're offered a job none of us is available to take.

Not long ago, Dawn went back to California to visit with her father. (Her parents arc divorced.) She'll be gone for several months. (We're hoping and praying she doesn't decide to stay permanently.) While she's gone, Shannon has taken her place and now comes to regular meetings.

Now that I've told you a little about our history, here's a quick rundown of the members. I'll start with Kristy since you already know a bit about her. As I said, she's president and founder of the BSC. Kristy also loves sports and could care less about fashion. Give her a sweatshirt, jeans, and a baseball cap and she's happy. Kristy is short and petite, but has a big personality (and an even bigger mouth). She is the most take-charge person I've ever met. She runs the BSC more professionally than some businesses are run. She also runs a kids softball team called Kristy's Krushers. (Their biggest rivals are a team called Bart's Bashers run by Kristy's sort-of boyfriend Bart Taylor.)

Not long ago, Kristy's family life underwent a dramatic change. You see, Kristy's mother had been raising Kristy and her three brothers (she has two older ones named Charlie and Sam) ever since her father walked out on them. That was right after David Michael was born. I'm sure it was tough for Kristy's mom, but she was managing to keep everything together. Mrs. Thomas had a good job at a big company in Stamford (the closest city to Stoneybrook). Then she started dating a guy named Watson Brewer whom she'd met at work. They fell in love and got married.

That alone would be dramatic enough. But, get this. Although Watson looks like your average, quiet guy, he's actually a millionaire. Suddenly Kristy and her family were rich. They packed up and moved to Watson's gorgeous mansion on another side of town. (Kristy used to live in an average kind of house across from my average kind of house here on Bradford Court.)

The dramatic changes didn't stop there, either. Kristy had to get used to her new younger stepbrother and sister, Andrew and Karen. They're Watson's kids from his former marriage. Even though most of the time they live with their mother and her new husband, they still spend every other weekend and some holidays and vacations with Kristy's family. That's fine by Kristy. She's crazy about Karen and Andrew and they feel the same way about her.

As if this weren't enough change, Watson and Kristy's mother adopted a baby who was born in Vietnam. Emily Michelle is two-and-a-half and totally cute. Since Watson and Kristy's mom both work, Nannie (Kristy's grandmother) came to live with them to help care for Emily Michelle.

With all those people (as well as assorted pets), Kristy's house is always hopping. But if anyone can handle it, it's Kristy.

Speaking of dramatic family changes brings me to Mary Anne and Dawn. Their story is even more interesting than Kristy's. Mary Anne and Dawn are not only friends, they're stepsisters. But they started out as just friends. I'll begin their story by telling you about Mary Anne. She lived with her father next door to Kristy in another average kind of house. Her mother had died when Mary Anne was a baby and her father was very strict with her, always treating her like a little kid.

Mary Anne and Kristy were best friends almost from the time they were born. They even look a little alike, both petite with brown hair and eyes. (Only now Mary Anne's hair is short, so they don't look quite so much alike.) However, unlike Kristy who lets you know exactly what she's thinking at the exact moment she thinks it, Mary Anne is quiet and shy. She's a good listener and very sensitive. She cries easily over anything sad.

Anyway, one day in the seventh grade, Mary Anne befriended a girl who had just moved to Stoneybrook from California. That was Dawn. Mrs. Schafer, Dawn, and her brother, Jeff, had moved here because Mr. and Mrs. Schafer had gotten divorced. Mrs. Schafer was originally from Stoneybrook so she came back after the divorce to be closer to her parents. But the move was hard on Dawn and even harder on Jeff. He missed California and his dad so much that he went back to live with his father. That left Dawn with half her family on one coast and half on the other.

Dawn and Mary Anne hit if off right away despite their differences. (They're pretty different, too.) Dawn is tall and slender with long, white-blonde hair and blue eyes. She has her own casual style of dressing. Dawn is very independent, a real individual who does what she thinks is right no matter what anyone else thinks.

Anyway, Mary Anne and Dawn were looking through Mrs. Schafer's old high school yearbooks when they discovered that Mary Anne's father and Dawn's mother had been boyfriend and girlfriend in high school. Mary Anne and Dawn came up with the bright idea of getting their parents back together, and it worked! After an eternity of dating they finally got married.

Mary Anne and her father went to live with the Schafers in their old (1790) farmhouse. It's a great house (not average at all) that even has a secret passage which runs from Dawn's bedroom out to the barn in the back. The house was part of the underground railway which helped slaves escape from the South to the North.

Becoming a new family wasn't as easy as Dawn and Mary Anne had expected. For instance, there was a problem with food. Dawn and her mother only eat healthy things such as tofu and bean sprouts, and absolutely no meat. I can't imagine life without junk food, fast food hamburgers, and french fries. But the mere thought of any of that stuff would make Dawn want to hurl. Mary Anne and her father eat normal food so it was hard putting

17

meals together at first. Now they've adjusted to each other and, despite their rough times, are happy to be a family. (I know Mary Anne misses Dawn like crazy. She took Dawn's leaving hard, although, since she's so understanding, she's trying to understand how much Dawn missed her father and brother.)

My friend Stacey McGill has had more than her share of adjustments to make, too. She moved here to Stoneybrook from New York City in the seventh grade. She's much more sophisticated and grown-up than any of us. (I know my friends think I'm sort of sophisticated, too, but if you ask me, I'm nothing like Stacey.) Anyway, Stacey has huge blue eyes, and blonde permed hair. Like me, she *adores* clothing and has a great sense of style. Unlike me, she's a good student, especially in math where she's a whiz.

Stacey keeps such an upbeat attitude that you'd never guess how many tough things she's had to deal with. Tough thing number one: her health. Stacey has a very serious form of diabetes, which is a disease in which her body can't properly regulate the amount of sugar in her system. If she doesn't watch her diet (absolutely no sugar or junk food) and give herself insulin injections every day, she could go into a coma. I admire how disciplined she is in sticking to all this and how she doesn't let it get her down.

Tough thing number two: the number of times she's had to move. First she moved to Stoneybrook, which wasn't easy since she missed New York City and her friends there. Then, once she'd made new friends here (us) her father's company transferred him *back* to New York. By then, Stacey wasn't thrilled to return because she'd come to think of Stoneybrook as her home. She didn't have any choice about it, though, so back she went. Once she was in Manhattan, something else happened which leads me to Stacey's third tough thing.

Tough thing number three: Stacey's parents' divorce. Stacey had to decide whether to stay in the city with her father or come back here with her mother. Luckily for us, she came back here.

Another BSC member who made a difficult move is Jessi. Just like Stacey, she moved here because her father's job changed. I suppose all moves are difficult, although I wouldn't really know since I've lived here on Bradford Court for all eternity. For Jessi, moving was particularly hard because it gave Jessi her first real experience with prejudice. Her old neighborhood had been pretty integrated, but Stoneybrook is mostly white. Some of the neighbors weren't thrilled when a black family moved to the neighborhood, and they made their feelings known.

Not long ago, I encountered a family who didn't want me to sit for their kids because I'm Japanese-American. It really shocked and hurt me, especially since I'd never experienced anything like that before. So I can imagine how awful Jessi and her family must have felt. The Ramseys aren't quitters, though, and they hung in there. Now things are much better, and the Ramseys — Jessi's mom and dad, her baby brother Squirt and eight-year-old sister Becca, and her aunt Cecelia — have made some good friends and neighbors.

Jessi is pretty remarkable. Sometimes she reminds me of a deer with her thick lashes and dark eyes, her long legs and graceful movements. Of course she's not a deer, but she is a ballet dancer, and a talented one. She studies regularly at a ballet school in Stamford and has already performed in several professional productions.

Jessi's best friend is Mal Pike. Mal is the oldest of the eight Pike children which may be why she's so good with kids. She has a great imagination, too. She wants to be a children's book writer and illustrator. I think she'll be great at it. She even looks like my idea of an author with her glasses, brownish red curly hair that tumbles where it wants to go, and her serious expression (which she wears until she breaks out into a great smile). Mal's snappy sense of humor is something I also imagine an author having. It's easy for me to imagine Mal's photo on the back of a book jacket. (Her braces don't quite fit the author picture, but they'll be gone by the time she publishes her first book.)

Recently Mal had a case of mononucleosis which left her so rundown that her parents have temporarily forbidden her to participate in any after-school activities, including the BSC. With Mal out sick and Dawn in California, we were really having a hard time covering all our jobs. Thank goodness Shannon agreed to come to meetings.

I should tell you a little about Shannon, although I don't know as much about her as I do the others. She's on the short side with blue eyes and curly, blonde hair. I suppose she must be wealthy since she lives in Kristy's new neighborhood where all the houses are gigantic, but she's not snobby. She has a good sense of humor and she must be smart since she's in her school's honor society. (She doesn't go to Stoneybrook Middle School like the rest of us.) Shannon is the oldest in her family and has two sisters, which means she's used to being around kids.

Oh, one more thing. I should tell you how the club works. As you know, we meet each week at a regular time and take phone calls. Mary Anne is the club secretary and her job is to keep a record book with everyone's schedule in it. My art lessons, Mal's orthodontist appointments, and Jessi's ballet classes are all in there. That way Mary Anne knows who is free to take the baby-sitting jobs that come in. Mary Anne is great at it. She keeps us organized. She also records information about our clients in the book. All their names, addresses, and phone numbers are there as well as the kids' fears, food allergies, or other important information.

We do much more than just take phone calls, though. For instance, at this meeting, Stacey was reminding us about club dues on Monday. No one ever wants to part with her money, but Stacey is the treasurer so it's her job to collect the dues and then decide how we'll spend it. Each month, part of the money goes toward my phone bill. (I'm vice president since we use my room and my phone.) Some of the money pays Charlie Thomas to drive Kristy here (and now Shannon, too). From time to time we also restock our Kid-Kits. Each of us has a Kid-Kit, which is a box full of small toys, coloring books, storybooks, and things like that. It was Kristy's idea to bring these kits with us on jobs, and kids love them.

Stacey works hard to keep track of how our dues are spent, but since she's such a whiz with numbers she does it well. So well, in fact, that once in a while there's money left over to do something fun like have a sleepover or go to the movies.

The other thing we do at meetings is read or write in our club notebook, which was another great Kristy idea. (At this meeting Jessi was busy writing about her last job with the Papadakis kids.) In the notebook we record everything about our baby-sitting jobs (and everyone complains about my spelling!). It's a pain to do, but it's a great reference when you're going to a new job or need to know what's going on with the regular clients.

Just so you know, when Shannon replaced Dawn she became the alternate officer, which means she has to learn everyone's job in case anyone is out sick or on vacation, although Mal and Jessi don't have special responsibilities as junior members.

With all the things we have to do at each meeting the time zooms by. And today the phone kept ringing and ringing. Just as Jessi handed the club notebook to me, the phone rang with a call from one of our regular customers, Mrs. Barrett.

"I'll see who's available and call you right

back, Mrs. Barrett," said Kristy, which is the usual way we handle jobs. She hung up and looked at Mary Anne. "Mrs. Barrett needs a sitter for this Tuesday at three-thirty. It will just be Suzi and Buddy. She's taking the baby."

Mary Anne opened the record book to Tuesday's schedule and studied it. "Why is she taking Marnie?" she asked.

"Marnie has an appointment with the allergist," Kristy told her. "Apparently she's been coughing and sniffling a lot."

"Maybe it's just a cold," Shannon suggested.

"Mrs. Barrett said it's lasting too long and Marnie's eyes are watering a lot," Kristy replied. "This is her second visit to the allergist. The last time she took Buddy and Suzi with her to the doctor, they got too fidgety and wild in the waiting room, so she wants to leave them at home."

"I don't blame her," said Stacey, laughing. "I wouldn't want to be stuck in a waiting room with those two."

"They're good kids, though," added Jessi.

"You sound like Dawn," I said with a smile. Dawn knew the Barrett kids best, and often volunteered to sit for them. But even *she* named them the Impossible Three at first.

"Claudia, you and I are the only two available that day," Mary Anne said.

"If you don't mind, I'd rather not," I told her. "I have a history test on Wednesday, and if I don't do well, I'm doomed."

"Mary Anne, you take it, then," Kristy jumped in anxiously. My grades are important to Kristy, since my parents have threatened to make me quit the BSC if it took too much time from my studies.

Mary Anne rolled her eyes at Kristy. "I was *going* to take it," she said, writing her name into the book. "You know," she added thoughtfully, "I was thinking. Isn't Marnie allergic to chocolate?"

Each of us looked to the other to see if anyone remembered. No one did, so Mary Anne flipped to the back of the record book to check. "Yup," she said, "she's allergic to chocolate."

"Mrs. Barrett wouldn't forget *that*, though, would she?" Shannon asked.

"I wouldn't be so sure," said Kristy. "She can be *awfully* scatterbrained." (Which was true.)

"She's much better these days," Mary Anne said. "I think she's trying to impress Franklin."

Franklin is Mrs. Barrett's new boyfriend. (Mrs. Barrett is divorced from Mr. Barrett.) The idea of older women, especially mothers, having boyfriends always seems just a little odd to me — although I know it's not. I mean, can you imagine? Scatterbrained and old (she was at *least* thirty as far as I could tell), Mrs. Barrett with her three wild kids had a boyfriend, and I didn't.

But if she'd found Franklin (and Kristy's mom had found Watson, and Dawn's mom had found Mr. Spier) then someone *had* to be out there for me. The trick was finding him.

CHAPTER 3

"Claud," Stacey said thoughtfully as she lay on a sleeping bag on my bedroom floor late that same night.

"Hmmm?" I replied absently. I was stretched across my bed and the two of us were paging through a stack of fashion magazines. I expected her to ask me if I thought a certain hairstyle in a magazine would look good on her, or if I liked a pair of jeans.

"What were you writing about when I came in this afternoon?"

I looked up from the story about a girl and her boyfriend which I was reading in *Seventeen*. "Why do you want to know?"

"I guess because you don't ever keep secrets from me, so I'm worried. Is everything all right?"

I smiled at her. Stacey is a great friend. "It's no big secret," I said. "I was making a list of qualities I would want in the perfect boy-friend."

Stacey looked relieved. "Oh. I thought it was some horrible problem."

"No. But sometimes it seems like one."

"What does?"

"Not having a boyfriend," I admitted. "I mean, you and Mary Anne are so lucky to have found boyfriends." Not long ago, Stacey started going out with this really cool guy at school named Robert.

"Robert is great," Stacey said dreamily. "But don't worry, Claud. You'll find someone, too."

"Well, why haven't I?" I demanded. "Even Kristy has Bart. Sort of."

Stacey rolled onto her side and rested her cheek on her hand. "Do you know what I think your problem is?"

"I'm fatally unattractive to the opposite sex."

"Claudia!" Stacey wailed. "You are extremely attractive, and maybe *that's* your problem."

"What is?" I asked doubtfully. "That I'm *too* attractive? Give me a break!"

"No, I'm not kidding," Stacey insisted. "I think a lot of guys might be intimidated by you. You're so pretty, and you're so much more mature than most of the boys. I don't think they would have the nerve to ask you out."

"So, what do I do?"

Propping her chin on her hand, Stacey narrowed her eyes in thought. "You need to let guys know you're looking for someone, but not just any guy. Someone who's the right guy for *you*."

"That sounds fine, but how do I accomplish this feat of mental telepathy? For that matter, how do I even find this guy?"

"I don't know," Stacey admitted. "Can I see your list?"

"All right." I dug under my bed for the stationery. "Tell me if you think it's dumb," I said, handing Stacey the list.

With a serious expression, Stacey read over the list. "A good talker *and* a good listener," she said.

"*You* are," I pointed out.

Stacey smiled for a moment and then frowned. "But a lot of people aren't. They seem to do either one or the other."

"What about Robert?"

"He talks a little more than he listens," she said. "But he comes pretty close to being in the middle. So, I suppose you can get both from people." She continued reading. "This guy sounds pretty wonderful," she commented when she was done.

"Shouldn't I want someone wonderful?" I asked.

Stacey sat up and thought about that. "Yes," she said. "Yes, you should. I think you're absolutely right to set high standards. So many girls settle on any old guy just so they can have a boyfriend. I don't understand how they can do that. Your guy will come along."

"Yeah, probably when I'm about fifty," I said glumly.

"Well, if that's how long it takes then that's how long it takes."

"Easy for you to say," I told her. "You have Robert right now."

"That's true," she agreed. She sighed deeply and so did I. Then we went back to our magazines. I had just reached the part in the story where the girl couldn't choose between two different great guys (lucky her) when Stacey sat up straight. "Look at this!" she said excitedly. "This might be the answer to your problems!"

"What is it?" I asked. She handed me her magazine open to a section which was full of small boxed-off sections. On the top was the word "Personals" and in the boxes were little advertisements sent in by the magazine readers. I read one of them out loud. "Gorgeous, intelligent, accomplished, blonde woman, thirtyish, seeks attractive, non-smoking man in same age range for theater, long walks, and possibly marriage. Must be successful, independent, and humorous."

"It sounds like she's looking for the same guy you are," Stacey commented.

"No way. I don't want someone thirtyish," I said. "And if this woman is so wonderful why does she have to advertise for a date?"

"You're so wonderful and you're looking," Stacey replied. "Maybe this woman is shy and doesn't meet a lot of men. Or she has to stay home and take care of her ancient father or . . . or . . ."

"Or she has the personality of Homer Simpson," I suggested.

"Not necessarily. Look at how many ads are in this magazine. This is just another way to meet people, like a do-it-yourself dating service."

I read some more personals to myself. Someone named Bob wanted to wish his wife a happy anniversary. (I don't know why he couldn't have just done that at home with a card.) A woman named Annette wanted to locate her old college roommate, Trudie. (That I could understand.) A guy named Dave wanted to hear from anyone who collected and might want to swap old comic books. But most of the ads were placed by people looking for a date.

Some of the people sounded as if they had a good sense of humor. One said: "A little bald, short, and shy — at least you know that I don't lie. Hope to meet Ms. Perfect, you. But Ms. Pretty Good will do, too. Send letter to Vernon."

Most of the people sounded too good to be true. They described themselves with words like *beautiful*, *amazing*, and *incredible*. "This sounds like the place where egomaniacs write in to meet other egomaniacs," I said to Stacey.

"I suppose nobody answers ads for people who are just *okay*," Stacey said.

"I guess. I wonder if anyone will answer the ad from 'A Little Bald,' " I said, showing her the ad. "He sounds sweet."

"Yes, he does, but would you answer his ad?"

"No," I admitted. "He's not exactly what I'm looking for."

"Well, there you go. That's why everyone writes all this great stuff about themselves. Everyone is looking for someone who is perfect. This guy is probably the nicest person in here, but he won't get a lot of replies."

"Yeah, well, I'm a little young to be going out with a bald guy," I argued, even though I knew what she meant.

Stacey made a face at me and returned to

the ads. "I'm trying to see if anyone in here would be good for you," she said as she read.

"Stacey! I'm not looking for some old guy!"

"I know that," Stacey replied. "I just thought someone young might have written in — but everyone in here seems to be old."

"Too bad the *SMS Express* doesn't have a personals column," I said. (I was talking about our school newspaper.) "Maybe Mr. Perfect is right in our school."

Stacey put down her magazine. Her blue eyes looked even wider and bigger than usual. "That's a *great* idea! Why don't you start a personals column? It would be a terrific addition to the paper and you could use it to find your Mr. Perfect."

"Me?" I laughed. "Me, the worst speller on the planet, work for the school newspaper? I don't think so. If they wanted an illustrator that might be different, but writing a column is not exactly what I'm good at."

"You could do it," Stacey insisted. "You wouldn't have to write much. You'd just have to collect the letters and organize it."

"I'd have to know if the letters had misspellings in them," I said.

"Emily Bernstein checks everything before the paper goes to print," said Stacey. Emily is the paper's editor, and is extremely smart.

"She'll fix any spelling mistakes."

"What if Emily doesn't want a personals column in the paper?" I asked.

"What if she just never thought of it before? I'll come in and help you with it."

"If you're so excited about it, why don't you do it?" I said.

"Because it was *your* idea."

"It was?"

"Sure it was. Anyway, you and Emily are friendly. You should mention it to her on Monday."

"I'll think about it," I said. I glanced at the clock and remembered that there was a great horror movie on TV. If we kept the sound low we could probably watch it without waking everyone else. Closing our magazines, we crept out of my room and down to the living room.

The movie wasn't nearly as scary as I'd expected. In fact, I fell asleep on the living room couch watching it and Stacey zonked out on the floor. We woke up to the sounds of my parents preparing breakfast. Looking like two zombies, we trudged up to my bedroom and slept until noon.

We might have slept all day if Stacey hadn't had to sit for the Hill kids (Norman and Sarah) at two o'clock. (With Mal temporarily out of action we were covering more day jobs than ever before.)

After Stacey left, I tried to study for my history test on Wednesday. Somehow I couldn't keep my mind on the beginning causes of World War Two. It kept wandering to Stacey's idea (or was it my idea?) about the personal ads. It might really work. And what better way to find Mr. Perfect? He'd know exactly what I was looking for. Anyone who didn't meet the requirements wouldn't answer the ad. At least the guys who answered would be close.

All day Sunday, I continued tossing the idea around in my mind. And the more I tossed, the better it sounded. By the time I woke up on Monday morning, I had made up my mind to talk to Emily about it.

I found her in the cafeteria at lunchtime. "Can I talk to you a sec?" I asked.

"Sure," Emily said, sitting down at an empty table. "What's up?"

I told her my idea of running an SMS personals column. Emily isn't one to leap on an idea. She takes it in slowly, so it's hard to tell what she's thinking. She just frowned and nodded as I spoke. But when I was done she said, "This might work out perfectly. We were thinking of getting rid of the half-page column on pet care. We've run through all the normal pets and now all that's left are weird ones like ferrets and snakes. Not too many kids have those. It wasn't so bad before we became a weekly paper, but now it's really hard to come up with new pet care ideas every week."

"I saw the article on caring for your parrot last week," I said.

"Did you read it?" Emily asked.

"No," I admitted. "I don't have a parrot."

"Neither does anyone else at SMS, but how many times can we write the same article about caring for your cat, dog, canary, or hamster? We really need something else in that spot, only no one has been able to think of what to put in its place. But now you've come up with something good."

"Then you want the column?" I asked excitedly.

Emily held up her hand. "*I* want it, but I have to run it past the rest of the staff. I'll let you know as soon as I can. We have a meeting this afternoon. I can call you later."

"Great," I said, getting up from my seat. "Thanks."

That evening, we were holding our regular meeting of the BSC in my room. Since the phone had been ringing for the entire half hour, I barely looked up from the BSC notebook, which I was writing in, when I heard it ring at five minutes to six.

"Baby-sitters Club, can I help you?" Stacey answered in the professional, polite way we always answer the phone during meetings. "Yes . . . this is Claudia's number. Oh, hi, Emily, this is Stacey McGill. . . . I'm fine."

At the sound of Emily's name I'd stopped writing and looked over at Stacey.

Stacey's face broke into a brilliant smile and she gave me the thumbs-up sign. "All right, I'll tell her. She'll be really happy. 'Bye, Emily."

I jumped off the bed. "She said yes?" I cried.

"What's going on?" asked Kristy.

"Claudia now has her own column in the *SMS Express*!" Stacey announced. "Emily said they're going to call it 'Claudia's Personals.' "

CHAPTER 4

Tuesday

Poor Marnie! She's a sniffling mess! Her eyes are running and she's wheezing. It's awful. No wonder Mrs. Barrett was worried. But when she came back from the allergist with Marnie she had a worse problem on her hands than she did before she went there.

Mary Anne went to the Barretts' on Tuesday. She was pleased to see that Mrs. Barrett had been keeping up with her get-organized campaign. The Barrett household used to look like a war zone, but no more. Mrs. Barrett has cleaned up her house, and organized the kids. You see, she went through a really tough divorce and for a long while that family looked like a tornado had hit it. Mrs. Barrett just couldn't handle it all. The kids were wild, the house was a horror, Mrs. Barrett would forget to tell her baby-sitters where she was going and she'd always return later than she'd said she would. Now things are a lot better over there.

Mary Anne couldn't help breaking into a big smile when she walked into the house. "Wow! The place looks great," she said.

"I keep trying," said Mrs. Barrett with a laugh. As she spoke, she scooped some magazines from the floor. "At least now I don't have to feel bad wondering if Marnie's allergies are caused by all the dust in this place."

"Is it her chocolate allergy?" Mary Anne asked as she put down her school books.

"No," said Mrs. Barrett. "She *never* eats chocolate." At that moment the sound of shouting came from the kitchen. Mary Anne and Mrs. Barrett rushed in to find Pow, the family's bassett hound, covered with Hawaiian Punch. Pow is a patient, good-natured dog. He just sat still and looked up with his big, brown eyes as the juice dripped over him. "It was an accident," said five-year-old Suzi.

"It was not," objected eight-year-old Buddy. "You grabbed my juice box right out of my hand."

"That's my juice box!" Suzi shouted. "I put it right down on the table for one minute and you took it."

As Mrs. Barrett knelt to wipe off Pow, Mary Anne got her first sight of Marnie who was sitting in her high chair looking red-eyed and miserable. "Poor baby," Mary Anne said, gently brushing Marnie's wispy blonde hair.

When the Hawaiian Punch mess was cleaned up, Mrs. Barrett lifted Marnie from her high chair. "Mary Anne, the number of the allergist is on the fridge. I should be home by five at the latest, so you don't have to feed the kids." (This really *was* the new Mrs. Barrett. Normally all she would have said was, " 'Bye," and swept out the door looking gorgeous, leaving the punch on the floor and probably even on Pow.) Mrs. Barrett put Marnie in her snowsuit and was about to leave when she stopped and added, "I almost forgot. If Franklin calls, please tell him it would be fine if he comes over with the kids around seven. That's very important."

"Sure," Mary Anne said, relieved that the DeWitt kids would be coming over *after* she was long gone. The Barrett kids and the DeWitt kids do not always get along. The kids are so concerned that their parents might get married that they often fight when they're together. (Mary Anne had been on hand when Franklin's kids visited the Barretts in their summer rental house at Sea City. She'd also baby-sat for the seven of them. She *knew* what a disaster the combination was.)

Luckily, Mary Anne wouldn't have to deal with that problem. And, with Marnie gone it was easy to keep an eye on Suzi and Buddy.

Once the Hawaiian Punch episode was over, the kids settled down to play a game together. They turned the living room into a make-believe zoo. Buddy placed his collection of rubber jungle animals across the floor, but Pow was the real star of the game. He got to play every animal in the zoo. Suzi put her dress-up ballerina tutu around his neck to make him a lion. Then she stuck a red clown nose on Pow's nose to turn him into Rudolph the red-nosed reindeer. (Suzi is convinced that red-nosed reindeers actually exist.) Pow even had to walk around with Buddy's white sweatshirt on when he was playing the part of a polar bear. The Barrett kids are lucky Pow is so easy-going. A lot of other dogs wouldn't have put up with a game like that.

After forty minutes of the zoo game, Nicky Pike, Mallory's brother, called on the phone for Buddy. He wanted to know if Buddy could come over, and Mal's little sister, Claire, wanted to play with Suzi. Mal got on the phone and told Mary Anne it was okay by Mrs. Pike. *"Please,* come over," Mallory begged Mary Anne. "Even though Mom's home she's doing a typing job for someone and I'm in charge of keeping my brothers and sisters out of her hair. I need some *normal* company."

Mary Anne thought about it a moment. "I'm supposed to wait for Franklin's call," she said.

"Turn on the answering machine," Mal suggested. "I think they have one. Mrs. Barrett could call him back later."

"All right," Mary Anne agreed. "I'll come over with the kids."

So Mary Anne turned on the answering machine, left a note for Mrs. Barrett, and bundled up the kids. They leashed Pow and took him to the Pikes' with them. When they arrived, Mal, Nicky, and Claire were waiting for them on the front lawn. The Pike triplets (Adam, Byron, and Jordan) were playing a game of touch football in the backyard, and Vanessa and Margo were playing hopscotch on the front sidewalk. "Mom said it was fresh air time," Mal explained, tucking one of her curls under her green wool beret. "Which means she couldn't work with all the noise in the house."

Mary Anne laughed as she clapped her gloves together for warmth. "It's not *too* bad out," she said. "And it's good for Buddy and Suzi to play outside. I'm sure Pow is happy."

"That's an understatement," Mal noted with a smile. The triplets had come around to the front and Pow barked happily as Byron threw sticks for him to retrieve. "He looks so funny when he runs," Mallory said, watching Pow waddle along at full tilt as he chased the sticks.

"He's a good dog," Mary Anne said, nodding.

"Thanks for coming over," Mal added. "If Mom and Dad don't lift the activity ban soon I'm going to lose my mind."

"How are you feeling?" Mary Anne asked.

"Fine! Well, almost. Some nights I'm pretty beat by the time I get to bed."

"Then maybe you still do need to take it easy."

"Yeah, but what good is being healthy if I'm completely insane by the time I get better?" Mal complained. "Plus, I miss you guys. Jessi tells me everything that's happening, but it's not the same."

"We miss you, too," said Mary Anne. "And it's hard now that both you and Dawn are gone."

"How's Shannon working out?" Mal asked.

"Fine. She's terrific. But she isn't you or Dawn."

From then on, the afternoon passed in a snap. Mary Anne and Mal hardly had to do anything since the kids were so busy playing with one another and with Pow. The Pike kids were thrilled with their visit from Pow since their only pet is a hamster.

Mary Anne was surprised when she looked at her watch and saw that it was already five to five. "Come on, kids," she called. "We've got to get home." The Pikes groaned and complained, but soon they said their good-byes and Mary Anne and her charges were off.

"So, how do you feel about the DeWitt kids coming over tonight?" Mary Anne asked as she and Suzi hurried along, trying to keep up with Buddy who was holding Pow's leash and was being dragged by the excited dog a bit faster than he could handle.

"Well, they're not as big toadheads as I first thought," Buddy conceded. "But I don't want them for brothers and sisters. I hope Mom doesn't marry Franklin."

44

"Don't you think it would be fun to be a big family like the Pikes?" Mary Anne asked.

"No!" Buddy said. "Besides we'd only be seven and the Pikes have eight."

"Maybe your mom and Mr. DeWitt would have another baby and then you'd have eight, too," said Mary Anne.

"Ew! Gross!" cried Buddy. "It's bad enough that we have Marnie."

"Marnie is not gross!" Suzi piped up.

"I didn't say that. I just said she's just a pain. That's all."

"She is not!" Suzi insisted indignantly.

The kids were still squabbling when they ran through the front door. They were so busy with their quarrel that they didn't notice the troubled look on Mrs. Barrett's face as she sat on the couch with Marnie on her lap. Mary Anne noticed, though. "How did it go?" Mary Anne asked cautiously.

Mrs. Barrett sighed deeply before answering. "The good news is that it's not anything that can't be cured," she replied. "The bad news is that she's highly allergic to cat and dog dander."

It took a moment for Mary Anne to comprehend what Mrs. Barrett was saying. "Does that mean she's allergic to Pow?" she asked.

"I'm afraid so."

"So, she'll just have to stay away from

Pow," said Buddy blithely as he and Pow played tug-of-war with an old facecloth.

"I'm afraid it's not that simple. Pow's hair is on everything in this house."

"We can clean it up," said Suzi.

"Dr. Reade says we have to get rid of Pow. There's no other way," Mrs. Barrett told them. "I discussed it with him at great length."

Buddy threw his arms around Pow's neck. "You're not killing my dog!" he shouted. "No!"

"Buddy, we would never do that," said Mrs. Barrett. "But we have to find a good home for him."

Suzi burst into loud sobs. Mary Anne put her hand on her shoulder and had to work hard to fight back her own tears. She knew that the last thing Mrs. Barrett needed was for her to start crying.

Buddy jumped to his feet, red-faced. "We've had Pow longer than we've had Marnie. Let's get rid of Marnie!"

"Buddy," Mrs. Barrett said softly, "I know that this is very difficult for you. It's hard for all — "

"I hate her!" Buddy screamed, pointing an accusing finger at Marnie who began to whimper.

"No one is taking my dog!" Buddy shouted again, his entire body quivering. Then he

46

jammed his palms in his eyes to dam up the tears and ran up the stairs. Crying loudly, Suzi ran up the stairs behind him.

The final straw came when Pow started to whine. Like Marnie, he didn't know what was going on, just that everyone was upset.

Looking as if she were about to burst into tears herself, Mrs. Barrett fished in her wallet and paid Mary Anne. By this time, Mary Anne was afraid that if she spoke she'd cry. With tremendous self-control she managed to say: "I'm sorry about Pow, but I'm glad Marnie will be better."

"Thanks, me too," Mrs. Barrett replied sadly. "And if you hear of anyone who would like a terrific bassett hound please let me . . ." That was all she said before she started crying, which was more than Mary Anne could stand. She burst into tears and found herself standing next to Mrs. Barrett and Marnie, all of them crying, while Pow whined along with them.

CHAPTER 5

In her own low-key, serious way, Emily Bernstein is a dynamo. She didn't waste an instant with "Claudia's Personals." I'm the kind of person who likes to let ideas sit around for a day or two until I get used to them. Not Emily. The moment I walked into school on Tuesday she practically pounced on me as if she'd been standing by the door waiting for me to arrive. (I think that's exactly what she had been doing.)

"Claudia, I am so excited about this," she said. She linked her arm through mine and started walking, talking with her head ducked down. I had to tilt my head down, too, to hear what she was saying. We must have looked as if we were exchanging top secret information.

"I've cleared off an old desk for you to use, and I've already marked a box for kids to drop their personals in," she explained. "We were extremely lucky because yesterday, once the staff voted to use the column, I was able to pull a little cartoon out of the paper and insert an announcement about your column."

"Wow!" I said. "You don't fool around."

Emily smiled. "You have no idea how fast you have to work on a weekly paper. Everything has to be done immediately. You'll see for yourself, once you get started."

I realized Emily had walked us to the *Express* office. Outside the door was a big cardboard box marked "Claudia's Personals" lined up with other boxes for things such as club announcements, finished articles, cartoons, letters to the editor, and sports schedules. All the other boxes were overstuffed with papers, but, of course, mine was empty. Then a horrible thought struck me. What if no one placed a personal ad? What if everyone thought the idea was just too strange? "I sure hope I get some ads," I said to Emily anxiously.

"I think you will," she replied. "And if you don't, it's back to 'How to Care for your Pet Iguana.' "

Inside the office were several desks, three computers, a photocopier, four typewriters, and an artist's slanted desk. "This will be your desk," Emily said, pointing to an old-looking, beat-up desk. I didn't mind the desk's condition. It was very wide and would be perfect for spreading letters out.

"How many letters can I pick?" I asked. "Assuming I get letters, that is."

Emily narrowed her eyes thoughtfully. "I'm pretty sure that space gives you two twenty-seven-line columns of forty characters each."

"Characters?" I repeated.

"Oh, that's editorial talk for letters of the alphabet. You can have forty letters in each line of your two columns." She narrowed her eyes again. "Or, you could run it straight across as one column of eighty characters. It would come out the same. Any way you want to do it is fine."

"Would you write that down for me?" It made no sense to me right now, but I figured I'd run it past Stacey, the math ace, and let her explain it to me. "Would it be all right if Stacey McGill came in and helped me?" I asked.

"Okay, but I'm depending on you to finish the column on time, and make sure it's right," said Emily.

"No problem," I agreed, although the sound of all that responsibility was scary.

"In the announcement I told the kids to include an address or phone number so we don't have to be involved with sorting through the responses to their ads. They can contact one another directly," Emily told me.

"Good idea," I said. I hadn't even thought about how that would work.

"As the editor, I read the entire paper before it goes to bed," she said.

"Before it does *what*?" I asked.

"Sorry, more newspaper talk. 'Goes to bed' means before it goes to the printer. Once it goes, no more changes can be made. We don't have the time to check over a test copy before the final printing. Since I'm the editor and the last one to see the paper before it's printed, if there's any problem I'm the one who gets blamed. But I'll need you to use your judgment and not put in any ads that are too weird."

"Do you think I'll get weird letters?"

"In my letters to the editor column I get some letters that I *know* are jokes, but I also get letters trying to gross me out, and once in a while a joke letter that some kid hopes I'll take seriously and print even though it's totally ridiculous."

"Like what?" I asked, really starting to worry.

"One time I got a letter from a kid saying that he had seen a cockroach in the cafeteria and that he felt that the only environmentally safe way to solve the problem was to let roach-eating gecko lizards loose in the cafeteria. He insisted that this should be put to a school vote immediately."

"Oh, gross!" I moaned. "I've never seen a roach in the cafeteria."

"Neither have I," said Emily. "And I wouldn't want to see a bunch of geckos crawling around, either. It was sent in by Alan Gray, and I'll bet he had a whole bunch of kids lined up to vote for gecko patrol."

"Alan Gray *is* a gecko," I said. At the very least, he was one of the most immature guys in our class.

"All I'm saying," said Emily, "is keep your eye out for anything that could cause trouble."

"Okay," I agreed. Just as the first bell rang, Emily showed me a photocopy of her announcement for Claudia's Personals. "The paper comes out tomorrow, so you'll be able to get busy right away," she said. Then she grabbed a schedule of deadlines as we rushed out of the room together toward our first classes. "Try to meet these deadlines," she said as we merged with a rush of kids. "It messes everything up if you're late."

The next day, I hurried to the *Express* office at lunchtime to pick up the new issue of the paper. Stacks of it were sitting outside the office door and I lifted one from the top. "There it is," I said to Stacey, who had come with me. I folded back the paper and showed her the announcement of my new column.

"Cool," Stacey said, reading it over. "You thought of this less than a week ago and here it is. Oh, and look at that!" Her eyes had traveled down to the cardboard box which had been set out in the hall for the letters for my column.

Three envelopes were sitting at the bottom of it!

"Already?" I cried as I stooped to gather up the envelopes. Excitedly, I ripped open the first one, a lavender envelope. Inside was written: "Roses are red, violets are blue, the BSC is real proud of you. Good luck with your new column. Love, All of Us." It was written in Mary Anne's neat handwriting. "Thanks. That's nice," I said to Stacey who was smiling. "Are the other two from you guys?"

She shook her head. "I don't think so."

The second ad was written in big, loopy handwriting. *I want to meet a cute, nice guy who is interested in hiking, animals, and camping. My friends say I am pretty but I still find it hard to talk to guys. Most guys don't even nodice me. I hope you do. (I'm in the 8th grade.) Write Shy Beauty at 12 Rose Court, Stoneybrook, CN, 10555.*

"This one is perfect," I said, handing the letter to Stacey.

"She spelled 'notice' wrong," Stacey pointed out.

"Do you honestly think I would know that? You promised to help me find spelling mistakes and stuff like that. Remember?"

"I will," she assured me.

"And I need you to look over the spacing stuff Emily was talking about. It's completely confusing."

"I'll help you, Claudia, I promise."

The next personal said: *Help! My parents are going Splitsville and it is messing up my head. Some days I feel like I'm going to explode with anger. Other days I want to crawl into a shell like a teenage, mutant, injured turtle. I want to find other kids with the same problem. I know you're out there. Maybe it would help to talk. Contact Sixth-Grade Sean with the Messed Up Life.* At the end he listed his address and phone number.

"What do you think I should do with this one?" I asked Stacey as I handed it to her.

"I sure know how he feels," said Stacey as she read it. "Poor kid. I suppose you could print it."

"I don't know. It seems too serious for this kind of column. My idea for Claudia's Personals was that it would be fun, maybe even a little silly."

"You can't just ignore something like this," Stacey pointed out.

"I know." I tossed the two letters back in

the box to look at later. "I'll have to think about it some more."

My column had just been announced and already I had a sneaking suspicion that I was in for more than I had bargained for.

CHAPTER 6

"Aughhh! It's an avalanche!" Stacey exclaimed two days later as we tried to keep the overflowing envelopes from sliding out of the box and onto the floor of the *Express* office. "Can you believe this?"

"It's pretty awesome," I agreed.

"And you were worried about getting mail," said Emily, joining us.

"I guess I didn't need to."

"You'd better get to it," Emily said cheerfully. "You've got your work cut out for you."

"Emily, we won't be able to use all of these," I said. "What should I do?"

"You'll have to pick the best ones and use them in the order they come in," she suggested. "If this keeps up, the staff will have to meet and discuss giving you more space."

As Emily walked away, Stacey grabbed my arm excitedly. "More space!" she whispered. "You're already taking over the entire paper."

"Don't get carried away," I said with a smile. "We might as well start reading these."

I thought choosing the letters would be a breeze. I would simply choose enough to fit the column and that would be it.

Wrong!

For starters, a lot of these kids didn't know the meaning of the word *short*. Emily's announcement had told them to place a *short* ad in the paper, but almost a quarter of the letters ran on for two pages. One girl went on for four pages! This is a bit of her letter: *I don't want to sound conceited because then you wouldn't like a conceited person, and I'm not conceited but it's very hard to write the good things about yourself without sounding stuck up, which I definitely am not. All my friends say I'm not. They even say I'm too unconceited which may be why boys don't notice me. That might be it, because otherwise I really am pretty noticeable. For one thing I'm large and I have purple hair! Not actually purple, of course, but purplish. I put in this eggplant henna rinse and it didn't exactly turn out the way I expected. I'm a big fan of Cleopatra and I wanted it to look like her hair. Let's just say I'm still working on it. I don't want you to think I'm fat (I could lose a few pounds I suppose). But mostly I'm tall and athletic. I'm on the girls basketball team and I like to play sports. My mother says big bones run in our family, so no shrimpy boys should answer. No offense to shrimpy boys but we might look odd together.*

This is how her letter went on for four pages! "This has got to be Liza Shore in the seventh grade," said Stacey after I told her to look over the letter. "No one else could fit this description."

"I *have* to shorten her letter," I said. "I'd hate not to use it after all the trouble she went to write it, but right now it would take up the whole column."

I took the letter home with me, and that evening I called the phone number Liza had included with her letter. "Hello, is this Big-Boned Beauty?" I asked, using the name which she'd signed to her letter. (I didn't want her to know I'd figured out who she was.)

"Yes," she answered cautiously.

"This is Claudia and I'd like to discuss your ad with you. It needs some work," I said.

Liza was agreeable and the next day after school I went back to the *Express* office and added Liza's ad to the column. *Unique, statuesque seventh-grade girl wants to get to know husky guy interested in sports and Ancient Egyptian cultures. For fun dates call Big-Boned Beauty at 555-7293.*

Liza hadn't been the only one I'd called that night. I'd called eight other kids about their letters. By the next day I'd turned a girl who had spent three paragraphs trying to explain how she hoped to find a boy who didn't mind a girl who talked a lot into: *Skilled communicator seeks strong, silent type boy for long, meaningful discussions. Contact Rambling Rose at the following address. . . .*

And the boy who went to great lengths (two and a half pages) to explain that he suspected girls wrongly thought he was a wimp just because he liked classical music and butterfly-collecting, was changed into: *If you love classical music and nature's beauty, this fun-loving boy seeks your company. Write to No Wimp at the following address. . . .*

"You're good at this," Stacey commented as we sorted through letters on Friday afternoon.

I blew a wisp of hair from my face. "I suppose, but it took me half an hour to figure out how to spell 'statuesque.' I was looking in the dictionary for something like 'staduesk.' I don't know how you're supposed to find the spelling of a word when you don't know how to spell it! It doesn't make sense. You know, Stacey, that's going to be the hardest part of this job."

"What is?"

"Spelling! I figured that the stuff kids sent in would be what we printed. I didn't expect to have to rewrite so much of it."

"Emily will fix your spelling," Stacey reminded me.

"I know, but I don't want her to think I'm an idiot. I told you working for a newspaper wasn't something I'd be good at."

Stacey looked thoughtful. Then she said, "Don't worry about it. I have something to show you which you're going to love."

Stacey moved over to one of the computers. "I talked to Emily before you got here, and she said we could use this to write up your column."

"But I don't know how to use a computer for writing," I objected.

"It's easy," said Stacey. "I'll show you. My dad's secretary has been showing me during my visits to his office." Stacey turned on the computer and opened a new file. "This will make your life so easy," she said. She typed in the sentence: *Staduesk butey sekes cule guy for fun daytes*.

"You spelled 'statuesque' wrong," I pointed out triumphantly. (The only reason I knew was because I'd just looked it up, of course.)

Stacey rolled her eyes at me. "Is statuesque the only spelling mistake you see there?" she asked in disbelief.

"Stacey, you know I'm not a good speller. Don't bug me," I replied, embarrassed.

"You'll be a good speller from now on," she said gleefully. She hit a button and the word *Spellcheck* came up on the screen, then, one by one all the misspelled words in Stacey's sentence were pointed out, the correct spellings were given, and they were even entered into the sentence. In minutes the sentence was correct.

"This is so cool!" I said excitedly. "This will change my whole life! It's beyond belief!"

"I don't know about changing your whole life, but as far as working on your column goes, you can check your spelling on this."

In an instant the impossible problem in my life had been nearly wiped away.

Up until now I had seen computers as interesting if they could be used for graphic design or pattern-making or something like that. Otherwise, I didn't have the slightest interest. But now I was seeing them in a new light. "This computer is the greatest invention on earth!" I said. "This spelling thing is, anyway."

"You have to learn how to use it first," Stacey reminded me.

"Oh, yeah." I pulled up a chair. "Let's get started."

Although other kids were in the office working on the paper, no one seemed to need our computer. So I sat and concentrated. Learning the commands wasn't easy but I was determined to master them. I discovered that I really liked working with the computer, too.

In fact, the time went so fast that I was shocked when Stacey showed me her watch.

"Five o'clock!" I shrieked, jumping out of the chair. "We have to get out of here!"

"We can make it," said Stacey, giving the computer several commands that would prepare it to be turned off properly.

"We can make it if we run all the way," I said as I grabbed my jacket.

Stacey and I flew out of the office.

CHAPTER 7

I avoided getting the Look from Kristy by a split second. (The Look is the deadly glare she gives to any club member who arrives late.) Stacey and I skidded into my room just in time to see the red digital number on my clock change from five-twenty-nine to five-thirty. Whew!

"Where were *you*?" asked Kristy, who is used to finding me here when she arrives.

"We were working on her personals column," Stacey explained as she took off her jacket.

"How is it going?" Mary Anne asked.

"Great," I said. "But it's not as simple as I expected." I explained how I had to reword a lot of the letters.

"Did you get the letter from us?" Kristy asked.

"I did. Thanks, you guys." Thinking of that letter reminded me of the other letters I'd received in that first batch, especially the one from the boy who wanted to form a support group for kids whose parents were getting divorced. Right now it was on my dresser since I'd taken it out the night before when I'd been making my phone calls. I just couldn't decide what to do about it. "I have a problem I'd like to run past everyone," I told Kristy. "Can we take a second to talk about it?"

"Sure, as long as the phone doesn't ring," Kristy agreed.

I read the letter to my friends. "This is much more serious than any of the other letters I've gotten," I told them.

"It does sound serious," said Jessi. "Maybe a group of kids talking about their feelings isn't a bad idea. I think you should print it."

"But is that enough? This kid sounds pretty messed up over this. What if he needs more help than a support group of kids can give him?"

"Maybe he should see a counselor," Mary Anne suggested.

"I thought of giving this letter to Sean's guidance counselor," I confided. "But I felt as if I'd be betraying his confidence."

"It's not confidential if he wanted the letter printed in the school newspaper," Kristy pointed out.

"I know, but he's turned to other students

for help, not to adults. Maybe he doesn't want to talk to someone older since his parents are adults. I don't know," I said, feeling pretty helpless.

"Seeing Dr. Reese helped me a lot," said Mary Anne. Earlier this year, Mary Anne was having a hard time. She was sorting through confusing feelings about some things, so with the help of her guidance counselor she started seeing Dr. Reese, a therapist. After seeing Dr. Reese for awhile, things seemed a lot clearer and more manageable to Mary Anne. Eventually, she stopped seeing her, but she says she hangs onto her phone number, just in case she feels the need to talk with her again.

"Dr. Reese," I repeated softly. "I wonder if Sean would go."

"You're not writing an advice column," Kristy reminded me. "If you try to solve everyone's problems you'll drive yourself nuts."

"I know," I admitted, "but something about this letter got to me. It was in my box the very first day. It's like Sean is desperate to find help somewhere. Look how fast he wrote the letter."

That's as far as the conversation went before the phone rang. The first call came from Mrs. Barrett. "Please, not me," said Mary Anne when Kristy asked who could take the job. "I can't face going over there again so soon. It's too sad. All I'll do is cry every time I look at Pow." She checked her book. The only other person besides Mary Anne who was available was Shannon.

"Sure, I'll take it," Shannon agreed glumly. "That poor dog."

"Those poor kids," added Mary Anne.

Shannon smiled sadly. "Them, too. But I guess I have a real soft spot for dogs."

Poor everybody! That's how I was feeling by the end of the meeting. I was bummed out about the Barretts, like the rest of the club members were. And I couldn't get Sean off my mind. Tomorrow was the deadline for my first column. I had to decide whether or not to print his ad.

When the BSC members had left, I sat on my bed and poured some letters out of a large manila envelope onto my bed. I picked up Sean's letter and tapped it on my hand thoughtfully. Then I picked up the phone and punched in the number he'd included in his ad. "Hi, can I speak to Sean, please?" I asked when a woman answered. "It's Claudia Kishi."

"Hello?" Sean asked anxiously.

"Hi, Sean, this is Claudia. I wanted to talk to you about your ad."

"Yeah?"

Suddenly this seemed like something I should do in person. "Could you meet me at the *Express* office Monday after school?"

"I guess so. Is something wrong with the ad?" He sounded incredibly nervous.

"No, not at all. I just want to talk to you about something. Okay?"

"Okay."

When I hung up, I had a sense of relief. Meeting Sean would help me decide whether I should offer him Dr. Reese's number, and then we could discuss whether he still wanted to run the ad.

Next, I put two letters in front of me. They were both from boys seeking girls. And, if you could believe what they said about themselves, they sounded pretty close to my Mr. Perfect. One said: *Eighth-grade boy seeks beautiful, interesting girl. I swim, sketch, and enjoy stand-up comedy. If this sounds good to you, I'd love to get to know you better. Call Good Listener at 555-3829, or write to this address. . . .*

He had a lot of the qualifications I needed. Swimmers have just the right kind of muscles, athletic without being overwhelming. If he sketched, of course he was artistic. The fact that he liked comedy meant he had a good sense of humor. Naturally, I'd have to meet him to see what he looked like, but he sounded good on paper.

The other letter said: *I'm a good-looking guy in the eighth grade. I'm looking for a girl who wants to share laughter, poetry, art, sports. Must be pretty, adventurous, funny, and a good dresser. Call 555-9000 or write Great Guy at my personal PO Box. . . .*

I was very intrigued by this letter, too. I was a little put off when he described himself as good-looking, but then, maybe he was just being honest. I mean, I know I'm pretty even if I don't go around saying it. Or maybe it simply meant that he was forthright and self-confident. Otherwise, he had almost all the qualities I was looking for. And the things he was looking for in a girl said a lot about him. If he wanted a funny girl he must be humorous then, himself, and if he valued a good dresser, then he obviously cared about fashion. Plus, I wanted to know why he had his own post office box. To me, that sounded very mysterious and sophisticated.

I'd put these letters aside with the idea that I'd keep them for myself and not print them. After all, I'd started this project so I could find Mr. Perfect. Didn't I deserve something for my efforts?

But as I sat on the bed, this very annoying feeling kept coming over me. It was the feeling that keeping these letters for myself wasn't ethical. Try as I did to push this guilty feeling away, it kept coming back.

"All right! I'll print them!" I said out loud to the air. (Or was I talking to the guilty feeling?)

That didn't mean I couldn't get a jump on the competition, though. I reached for the phone to dial Good Listener, but suddenly I felt funny about that, too. He might get a big head knowing I'd grabbed his letter out of all the others. (Since the paper hadn't even been printed yet, he'd easily figure that one out.) And I suspected that Great Guy might already be a little stuck on himself. This might send him over the edge. Plus, I felt too nervous to talk to a boy I'd never even seen. What if I babbled and sounded like a dweeb?

No. A letter would be better. It would be one of the first replies to arrive (so the guy wouldn't already be taken by the time I got there) but it wouldn't seem wildly over anxious.

Writing isn't my strong point, though. And you already know about my spelling. I decided to wait until Monday when I could use the Spellcheck on the *Express* office computer and ask Stacey to look it over for me.

Waiting wasn't easy, though. I almost went crazy that weekend composing the letter in my head. What did you say to someone you didn't know, yet whom you wanted to impress? "Hi, I think we're both great, let's get together and meet?" It wasn't an easy one to figure out.

Finally, Monday came. That afternoon I arrived at the *Express* office before Stacey did. I checked the sheet of directions she'd written out for me and got into the computer files. I was just beginning my reply to Great Listener when I realized someone was standing behind me.

"Hi, Emily," I said, suddenly wanting to cover the screen. I felt guilty about using the paper's computer for my own letters, but she wasn't looking at what I was writing. I guess she assumed it was my column.

"Someone is here to see you," she said, nodding toward the office door. Turning, I saw a slim, short boy with red hair and freckles. From the uncomfortable look on his face I knew he was Sean.

"Thanks," I told Emily as I got up and crossed the room to him. "Sean?" I asked when I reached him. He nodded, not meeting my eyes. "I'm Claudia. I'm glad you could come."

I led him over to my desk and offered him a chair. "Listen," I said as gently as I could, "this might be none of my business, but when I read your ad it seemed to me that you might want to talk to someone other than a bunch of kids."

"Like who?" he asked, confused.

I'd gotten Dr. Reese's phone number from Mary Anne over the weekend. I handed him the paper I'd written it on. "Dr. Reese really helped a friend of mine who was going through a hard time. My friend says she knows about kids and their feelings and everything."

"Did your friend's parents get divorced?" Sean asked, taking the paper.

"No, but her mother died and now she's part of a stepfamily," I told him. "Sean, I know a lot of kids whose parents have gotten divorced and it's not easy to deal with. There's nothing wrong with getting help in sorting out your feelings."

"That's why I wanted to form the group," he said.

"I can still run your ad if you want to," I told him. "I just had this number and I thought it might be helpful."

He looked down at the number in his hand. "Did my ad make you think I was crazy, like I really needed a shrink?"

"No," I said honestly. "But you sound like you're in a lot of pain."

He nodded. Then he stood up slowly. "Okay, thank you," he said and turned to go.

"Do you want me to run your ad?" I asked. He just shook his head. "Will you call Dr. Reese?"

His eyes looked a little red at the edges. He shrugged his shoulders and then left the office. As he headed out the door, Stacey came rushing in. "Was that Sean?" she whispered, sliding into the chair next to me. "How did it go?"

"I don't know," I admitted.

Stacey patted my shoulder. "You did the right thing," she assured me.

"I hope so," I said.

She picked up a pile of letters we'd agreed to run. "Come on," she said. "Let's type these up and put our very first installment of Claudia's Personals to bed."

With Sean still on my mind, I turned to the letters. "Okay," I said. "Let's do it."

CHAPTER 8

Tuesday

Boy! What a grim scene I walked into at the Barretts' house. Marnie looked okay, but everyone else looked completely miserable! Then something pretty unbelievable happened.

That Tuesday after school, Shannon arrived at "The House of Doom and Gloom," otherwise known as the Barrett house. When she rang the doorbell, Buddy pulled it open and scowled at her. "Oh, I guess Mom is going out again," was his greeting.

Shannon stepped in and was immediately met with the sound of a vacuum cleaner. Mrs. Barrett was vacuuming the living room rug, intent on giving Marnie a dust-free home so she can get better.

"MOM!" Buddy screamed at her over the roar of the machine.

Mrs. Barrett flipped off the cleaner. "Oh, hi, Shannon," she said. "I didn't realize it was four o'clock already."

"Where are you going *today*?" Buddy asked.

A guilty expression swept over Mrs. Barrett's face. "I'm going to meet another family who answered my ad," she said. (It seemed everyone was running ads these days.) "I know I've been going out a lot, Buddy, but I've been seeing a lot of people. So far no one has been right for Pow. We want him to go to the perfect place."

The stormy look on Buddy's face grew stormier and he stomped up the stairs. Mrs. Barrett shook her head as she untied her scarf, letting her hair swing loose. "I put an ad in the paper offering Pow to anyone who could give him a good home," she explained to Shannon.

"Does this family you're going to see sound good?" Shannon asked.

"I couldn't tell from one phone call. Franklin offered to take Pow, but we realized that if we ever merged our households, we'd just have to go through this all over again."

"Too bad," said Shannon sadly.

"Yes, it is. But there's no choice. Marnie can't go on suffering. At any rate, I've written down the number where I'll be. I don't think it will take more than a couple of hours at the most."

"How's Marnie?" Shannon asked.

"*Much* better since I put Pow in the garage," Mrs. Barrett replied. "Fortunately she's too little to realize that Suzi and Buddy aren't speaking to her. Although sometimes she pouts in a way that makes me think she knows something isn't right. The important thing is that her allergies have cleared up immeasurably. Once Pow is gone, I'm sure they'll improve even further."

"How is Pow doing?" Shannon asked.

"He whimpered all last night. He thinks he's being punished. Everyone will be happier once he's settled in somewhere else." Mrs. Barrett started up the stairs. "Come on. I want you to see the girls' room."

Shannon followed Mrs. Barrett upstairs and was astonished at the change in the room. The curtains had been taken down and the carpet rolled up. The big net that used to hang on the wall, crammed full of stuffed animals, had been taken away. The other stuffed toys were gone, as well. In the corner stood a bucket and a mop. The shiny floor looked as if it had been recently mopped. "The doctor said to keep this room as dust-free as possible," Mrs. Barrett explained.

"It looks like a prison cell!" complained Suzi who was playing on the floor with her Barbie doll.

"How would you know what a prison cell looks like?" Mrs. Barrett asked.

Suzi's hands went to her hips. "I saw one on *Teenage Mutant Ninja Turtles*. Shredder was in one and it looked just like this room."

Mrs. Barrett sighed as she lifted Marnie out of the crib. Right away, Shannon could see that she didn't look nearly as runny and miserable as she'd been when Mary Anne babysat.

"Did you have a nice nap, sweetie?" Mrs. Barrett said to Marnie.

Marnie smiled at her. "Nab, nab, nab," she

burbled. Then she caught sight of Suzi playing on the floor. "Dotty . . . dotty . . ." she called out, stretching toward Suzi.

"That's her word for dolly," Mrs. Barrett explained as she bent to put Marnie on the floor beside Suzi.

"Get her away from me!" Suzi cried, clutching her doll. "I'm not playing with a dog killer."

"Suzi!" Mrs. Barrett scolded, lifting Marnie back up. "We are not killing Pow. And it's not Marnie's fault. She can't help being allergic."

"Well, Pow can't help being a dog," Suzi snapped.

Mrs. Barrett shut her eyes, and looked as if she were counting to ten to regain her patience. Then she turned to Shannon. "Come on downstairs. We'll let Suzi play undisturbed in her prison cell."

Downstairs, Mrs. Barrett plunked Marnie in her high chair and took some noodles from the fridge. "Nuke these in the microwave for forty seconds," she said, and then went on to give Shannon a list of instructions so long that Shannon's head began to spin. "Don't let Marnie near Pow. If she gets very congested give her half a teaspoon of Benadryl which is in the medicine chest. If she won't take it in a spoon, there's a medicine dropper in the drawer by the sink . . ." And on and on it went.

Finally she left. As soon as the front door closed behind her, Shannon heard the sound of Buddy stomping down the stairs. He stopped at the kitchen doorway and scowled at Marnie. "I'm going *out* to the ga*rage* to be with my *dog.*"

"All right," Shannon said kindly. "But don't go too far from the house." Shannon felt horrible for Buddy. As he slammed out of the house, she brushed Marnie's soft hair. This was such a sad mess.

Shannon was feeding Marnie her noodles and butter when Suzi appeared and plopped down on a kitchen chair. "What if somebody like the Addams Family takes Pow?" she asked seriously.

Shannon smiled. "The Addams Family is nice, a little strange maybe, but nice."

Suzi's eyes went wide with horror. "No! Uncle Fester might chop off his head just for fun. Or the grandmother might cook him!"

"Suzi," said Shannon, "your mother won't give Pow to the Addams Family."

"She won't care. She just wants to get rid of him."

"That's not fair," said Shannon, wiping Marnie's chin with a napkin. "She's already turned down several families. She's not settling on just anyone."

At that moment, Buddy burst into the house, filled with excitement. Behind him was Nicky Pike. "Guess what?" Buddy shouted. "Nicky wants to take Pow!"

Shannon frowned. "Take him where?"

"Take him home, forever. To keep!" Buddy cried. "Isn't that great?! Then we can see him all the time. It will be like he's not even gone. Nicky says I could come over and walk him and everything."

"And me and Claire could play dress up and zoo with him just like always," Suzi added, dancing around the kitchen.

Nicky was grinning from ear to ear. The boys and Suzi were so elated that Shannon could hardly bear to disappoint them. But she figured she'd better point out the reality of the situation. "That's a great idea," she said. "But Mal always told me her parents think one hamster is plenty, what with eight kids in the house. I thought you had a strict no more pets rule, Nicky."

"Me and my brothers have been really begging for a dog," Nicky assured her. "Vanessa, Margo, and Claire have been helping, too. I think my parents have changed their minds."

"I wouldn't count on it," Shannon warned. "Nicky, you better check with your mother right now." Shannon figured that the sooner they heard the official no from Mrs. Pike, the sooner they'd forget the idea.

"Can I go with him?" Buddy asked.

"Okay, but call me when you've spoken to Mrs. Pike."

"All right," Buddy agreed, smiling. In a flash, he was out the door.

Shannon cleaned Marnie's face and then put on a Curious George video for the girls. She simply couldn't concentrate on playing with them until Buddy called. She knew he'd be upset when Mrs. Pike said no, and she was trying to think of the best, most consoling, thing to say to him.

The video was more than twenty minutes over before the phone rang. Shannon jumped up from the floor where she was sitting with Marnie and Suzi. "Hi, Buddy," she said snapping up the phone. "Listen, don't feel too bad because — "

"It's all set," he interrupted her happily.

"What?"

"Mrs. Pike said they could take Pow!"

"She did?" Shannon asked in surprise. "Are you sure?"

"Sure I'm sure."

"Can I talk to Mrs. Pike?" Shannon asked, wondering if Mrs. Pike was really even there.

"Okay," said Buddy.

In a minute Mrs. Pike came on the line. "Hi, Shannon. Yes, it's true. We'll take Pow as soon as we can get our backyard fenced in, which should be pretty soon."

"Great," Shannon said. "That's so great!"

"The other day when Mary Anne brought Pow over I took a break from my work and walked to the window. When I saw how well Pow was playing with the kids, and how happy they were with him, I thought if we could find a dog like Pow maybe I'd rethink my rule. Then when I discovered we could actually have Pow and help the Barretts out too, well, it seemed too good to be true."

"And you won't have to worry about getting stuck walking him," Shannon pointed out. "I'm sure Buddy will volunteer any time you need him. Suzi, too."

Mrs. Pike laughed. "Having two extra dog-walkers is fine with me. I think this will work out perfectly. Please have Buddy's mom call me when she gets in, all right?"

"Of course. She'll be so happy." Shannon said good-bye and hung up. "Pow is going to the Pikes'!" she announced to Suzi as she walked into the living room.

"Hurray!" Suzi cried, turning a backward somersault on the carpet. "Now we can see him all the time." She stood up and did a lopsided cartwheel. "I'm so happy," she said, flopping on the floor.

While Marnie continued watching Curious George, Suzi and Shannon lay on the floor and played Memory. All the while they talked about how Suzi would be able to visit Pow and bring him treats. "When I'm a little older I can sleep over with Claire and then I can even sleep with Pow all night," Suzi said.

An hour later, Mrs. Barrett returned. As she heard the door open, it suddenly occurred to Shannon that maybe Mrs. Barrett had already promised Pow to someone else. She hoped not. And when she saw Mrs. Barrett's glum face she wasn't sure what it meant. Was Mrs. Barrett sad because Pow was going, or because he wasn't going? "What happened?" Shannon asked anxiously.

"No good," Mrs. Barrett reported, tossing her purse onto the couch. "The couple already has five dogs which they keep in a pen. Pow just isn't used to that kind of outdoor life. Plus, I didn't know how he'd do with those other big dogs."

"That's terrific!" Shannon cried.

Mrs. Barrett looked at her as if she'd lost her mind. "Excuse me?"

"Wait until you hear this," Shannon said. "You tell her, Suzi."

"The Pikes are taking Pow!" Suzi shouted,

and with that she jumped up and wrapped her arms around her mother.

Mrs. Barrett's weary face spread into a radiant smile. "Thank goodness," she said, smoothing Suzi's hair. "Thank goodness."

CHAPTER 9

Describing yourself is *not* easy! That's what I was discovering as I tried to come up with replies to the two personal ads that interested me.

The night that Claudia's Personals "went to bed" — I didn't. I was determined to stay up until I had written a letter which expressed the real me. (I hadn't been able to get onto the computer again to write my letter. I decided I'd compose it at home and then rewrite it on the computer.)

By ten o'clock, with my eyes starting to close, this is what I had come up with. *Hi. My name is Claudia. You sounded grate in you ad. I dont no if you no who I am from skool, so I gess I shuld describe myself. I have long, black hare and I like fashun. Some peepul say I'm pretty. I love art, mystury books, and junk food. It wuld be grate to meet you.*

Yuck!

Wasn't there more to me than that? It sounded so uninteresting. I mean I don't just love art. I LOVE art! I can't look at a sunset without thinking about the best way to get that same effect with watercolors. I can't even pick up a wad of Play-doh when I'm baby-sitting without wanting to sculpt the face of the kid I'm sitting for. Art is who I am.

But how could I write that in a letter to a guy I don't know without sounding like a complete maniac? I didn't want him to mark my letter, "obvious nut case," and throw it in the trash.

Even though I didn't have the guts to write about my intense love of art in my letter, I was dreaming of finding a guy I could tell it to. Or, even better, someone who would know that and so many other things about me without my saying a word.

I crumpled my letter and threw it under my bed. I tore another piece of paper from my spiral notebook and started again.

Claudia here. Let me tell you about myself. I'm good-looking, pashionate about art, like laffter, freinds, and I want too meet sumone who will like me as I am and not try to change me. From your ad I got the idea we mite have a lot in comon. There is nuthing to lose by finding out. Sincerly, Claudia Kishi.

It wasn't a whole lot better, but it would have to do.

The next day I went to school early and wrote my letter on the computer. (Wow! Had I ever spelled a lot of words wrong. The Spellcheck was going wild.) I printed two copies of the letter and put each one in a stamped, addressed envelope. Then I ran outside and dropped them into the mailbox by the front door.

Done. Now all I could do was wait.

On my way to class, Emily Bernstein caught up with me in the hall. "Claudia, we've actually run out of copies of the paper," she said. I wasn't sure if this was good news or bad, but Emily seemed overjoyed, so I supposed it was good. "This has never happened before!" she went on.

"Why?" I asked. "I mean, why have you run out of copies? Did you make too few?"

"It's because of your column!" she cried. "We printed the same amount as always, but this week everyone is dying to read the paper. All the kids are talking about it. This issue practically disappeared within a half hour."

"It did?" I said. "And you think that's because of the personals column?"

"I'm sure of it. I'm surprised you haven't heard kids talking. What have you been doing this morning?"

I was too embarrassed to tell her the truth — that I'd been using the *Express* computer to respond to ads in my own column. "Nothing," I said. "I just hadn't heard anything about it."

"You will," Emily assured me. "Good work. At lunchtime I'm going to put an extra box out in the hall to hold all the ads I expect to come flooding in. We definitely have to give you more space in the paper."

"This is pretty exciting," I said. Exciting and a little unnerving. There's something overwhelming about being responsible for a mountain of mail.

It wasn't long before I discovered for myself that what Emily had said was true. Everywhere I went that day, kids had the *Express* spread out in front of them. And those who didn't seemed very intent on writing in their notebooks. I had the strange suspicion that they were all composing ads to put in Claudia's Personals.

Not only was my column a huge hit (or "a phenomenon" as Emily called it that afternoon at lunch) but overnight I had become a celebrity. As I walked down the hall I noticed kids pointing me out to their friends. "That's her," I heard a bunch of sixth-grade girls whisper as I went by. It was fun. Yet, as I looked at all the faces looking at me, I mostly just wondered which of them was Great Guy and which was Good Listener. I hoped I'd hear from them soon.

As it turned out, I did hear from them pretty quickly, although at the time I felt as if I'd waited an eternity. On Thursday evening, right after supper, my phone rang. "Hello, Claudia," a boy's voice said when I answered. "Guess who this is?"

His voice was familiar, but I couldn't put a face to it. "I don't know," I said.

"It's me, G.G."

G.G? G.G.? I searched my brain for someone with those initials. "Great Guy?" I asked.

"Give the lady a prize! You got it. I got your letter this afternoon and I think you're absolutely right. We do have a lot in common."

"Do you know who I am?"

"You bet I do."

"Who are you?"

"Just one great guy. How about meeting me tomorrow after school? We can go to a movie. Or maybe play some video games."

"I'm not big on video games," I confessed.

"If you want to have a lot in common with me, you have to love video games," the boy said.

I didn't like his cocky attitude already. That's when it hit me (like a sledgehammer). I did know this voice. Only, I really hoped the owner of the voice wasn't who I thought it was. "I don't want to offend you or anything if you're not him but — is this Alan Gray?" I asked.

"You guessed it!" He laughed.

Alan Gray! Ew! Ick! I'd actually written to the most obnoxious, immature boy in the entire eighth grade! How mortifying!

"Tell me, Claudia, what impressed you most about my ad?" he asked.

"The post office box," I lied. "How did you get a post office box?"

"It's my dad's. He runs a mail order business from our house and he doesn't want all the customer mail coming there."

"Oh," I said. "Well, it's been nice talking to you."

"Hey, wait a minute. What about our date?"

"Are you serious, Alan?"

"Sure. You answered my ad didn't you?"

Alan may be a major dweeb, but there was no reason to be rude to him. So I said, "Alan, I can't go out with you because I already know a girl who is crazy about you."

"You do?"

"Yes," I said. "She'd really feel betrayed if I went out with you since she's confided how she feels to me. If I'd known the ad was from you I'd never have written since this other girl really can't wait to go out with you. You understand how it is."

"Who is this other girl?"

"I can't tell you, but I'm sure you'll be getting a letter from her very shortly," I said. (Which was true. Someone was bound to answer his ad.)

"All right. I understand," said Alan. "So long."

"So long."

Whew! Thank goodness I'd found a way to wriggle out of that one. Not only would a date with Alan Gray have been a nightmare, but I'd have wanted to die if anyone had seen us together.

I didn't hear from Good Listener until Friday night. "Hi, Claudia, this is Brian Hall. You might know me as Good Listener."

"Hi," I said. I had a sort-of idea who Brian Hall was. At least I knew what he looked like. He'd come to SMS at the end of seventh grade and he wasn't in any of my classes this year, but I knew he was very cute — tall with sandy blond hair and an athletic build.

"I got your letter this afternoon and I was pretty excited to hear from you."

"You know who I am?"

"Sure, since your column came out everyone knows who you are. But I've known who you are for awhile. I've always wanted to ask you out, but since we don't know one another, I didn't know how to do it."

"Wow," I said, flattered.

"Anyway, when I got your letter I could hardly believe it. It was good luck, don't you think?"

"Absolutely," I replied. Good luck? No way. It was destiny. This was meant to be. It was so obvious.

"I was thinking we could meet at the Rosebud Cafe for lunch tomorrow," he said. The Rosebud Cafe is one of the coolest places in Stoneybrook. I adore it. It didn't surprise me that he'd picked it since I could tell he was Mr. Perfect. And Mr. Perfect was sure to pick the perfect place.

"Sounds great," I said. "What time?"

"One o'clock?"

"No problem. I'll meet you there."

"I can't wait," he said.

Neither could I.

CHAPTER 10

"Mom, you can't," I protested as my mother pulled up in front of the Rosebud Cafe the next day.

"I can and I will," Mom insisted. "I am sitting right here until you introduce me to this boy. That was the deal we made last night, Claudia. Or did you forget?"

"No, I didn't forget," I grumbled. You would think I was going to my prom instead of spending a Saturday afternoon at the Rosebud Cafe. "But it's not like this is even a date."

"Then what would you call it?"

"Meeting someone for lunch."

"Meeting a *boy* for lunch," she corrected me. "That's a date."

I sighed in exasperation and slumped down in my seat. This was going to be really embarrassing. What good was it that I'd spent hours putting together an outfit if my mother was going to make me look like an infant before the lunch even started. (I'd settled on a long white shirt under a green tapestry vest, green corduroy pants, and low boots.)

Just then I noticed Brian walking toward the front door of the Rosebud Cafe. "That's him!" I told Mom as I practically leapt out of the car.

Immediately I was hit by a blast of cold wind, although I hardly noticed it. I was *so* nervous! "Brian, hi," I said.

He smiled, and judging from his expression, he was a little nervous, too. "I know this is totally a drag, but would you mind saying hello to my mother? She's kind of insisting on it."

"Sure," he replied with a forced-looking smile. (Who could blame him for not relishing the idea?) He walked around to the driver's side of the car as Mom rolled down the window. "Hello, Mrs. Kishi," he said, extending his hand. "I'm Brian Hall."

Mom shook his hand and I could tell from her smile that she approved of Brian. Why not? He was the picture of clean-cut good looks. His hair was short and neat, but not too short. His clothes looked pressed. He even smelled lightly of cologne. "Pleased to meet you," Mom said. "You kids have a nice lunch. I'll be back for Claudia at two-thirty." With that, she rolled up the window and drove off to do some work at the library. (She's the head librarian at the Stoneybrook Public Library.)

"Thanks," I said to Brian.

"No problem. Let's go have some lunch." On the way in, he held the door for me and he helped me out of my jacket when we got inside. I was pretty impressed.

In fact, Brian's old-fashioned manners seemed to fit perfectly with the Rosebud Cafe's old-fashioned decor. With a little imagination you could pretend you were back in the 1940s. The cafe even has a real soda fountain.

The hostess brought us to a table. Brian pulled out my seat for me and then sat down himself. Looking at the menu and then ordering gave us something to do at first. (I ordered fries, a hamburger, and a milkshake. He ordered an egg salad sandwich on whole wheat bread and a glass of milk. Yuck!) But finally the moment came when we had to make conversation.

It was not easy.

For a half minute or so (the longest half minute of my life) we just looked at each other. Then I remembered he was a Good Listener, so I figured it was up to me to talk. "Where did you live before you moved to Stoneybrook?" I asked.

"In New York, on Long Island."

"Why did you move?"

"Dad changed jobs."

"What does your dad do?"

"He's an accountant."

"Oh. Does he like accounting?"

"I think so."

More silence. He smiled. I smiled. As I smiled, I tried desperately to think of something else to ask him. "Your ad says you like to sketch. So do I. What do you sketch?"

"Model cars mostly. I like to assemble them, too. Then I sketch them."

"What do you do with your sketches?"

"I keep them in a notebook so I can remember which cars I have in my collection."

"Is it hard to put together the models?"

"No, they come in kits. The directions tell you exactly what to do. They tell you what colors to paint them and where to put the decals. It's all there for you."

Where's the fun in that? That's what I was thinking, but, of course, I didn't know him well enough to say that. Here I thought I'd found this artistic guy, and he was sketching model cars which he put together with instructions! Not *exactly* what I had in mind. "Do you think you'd ever like to sketch anything else?"

"Yes, definitely."

"Oh, you would?" I said, brightening.

"Yeah. I'm thinking of getting into model jets. Then I would sketch those and start a separate book for them. I just bought a fighter jet kit but I haven't opened the box yet."

"I see," I said. But what I couldn't see was sitting around with some guy handing him little tiny plastic pieces and telling him, "This is piece one hundred and five, the back wing flap." It was *not* my idea of a fun or creative time.

Luckily, our orders arrived then. While I chewed, he neatly cut the crusts off his whole wheat bread. At least it gave us something to do. I hoped that since my mouth was full, he might attempt some conversation. He didn't.

"So, you like stand-up comedy," I said in between bites.

Brian nodded. "Yeah. I really like people who can make me laugh."

So did I. But neither of us was doing much laughing. I tried to think of something funny to tell him, but somehow I just wasn't feeling funny. I suppose it had been dumb of me to assume that because he liked comedy, he, himself, was funny.

Okay, so he wasn't really artistic and he wasn't funny. And although he was a good listener, he didn't appear particularly interested in me. *I* was the one asking all the questions. So far he hadn't asked me a single thing about myself. And since he didn't ask, I didn't feel particularly comfortable talking about myself. You only tell someone about yourself if they seem interested. (He hadn't even commented on my dangly Native American beaded earrings which he *must* have noticed. So much for finding a guy who was interested in fashion.) Even though the other boys I'd liked in the past hadn't been Mr. Perfects, they had been a whole lot easier to talk to than Brian.

And want to hear something strange? Brian was starting to look much less handsome to me. I noticed that his eyes were too close together. His nose which I'd originally thought was perfect, now looked too sharp. Even his straight mouth was beginning to look pinched. I also decided his muscles were too close to the bulgy sort I hated.

I sneaked a quick peek under the table at my purple plastic watch. It was only one-thirty! *What* were we going to talk about for another entire hour?

"I like to swim," I said, remembering he'd said he enjoyed swimming in his ad.

"Yeah, swimming is fun." He wiped some egg salad from his chin. "Do you race?"

"No, I never have."

"I was on the swim team back in Long Island. I was their best butterflier."

"Butterflier?"

"Yeah, you know, the butterfly stroke. You raise both arms at the same time, unlike the

Australian crawl where you alternate arms. It takes a lot of upper body strength and I've always been good in that area. I like to lift weights, too. I think it's important to keep in shape." That explained the too bulgy muscles.

The waiter cleared our plates and asked if we wanted dessert. I was stuffed, but I ordered some ice cream out of desperation. At least with food in front of us we'd have something to do.

Conversation dragged all through dessert. Brian wasn't a bad guy. He was nice and he did have interests, but he wasn't *my* Mr. Perfect. Not even close.

At about two-fifteen, I couldn't take it any longer. "I'd better get outside and wait for Mom," I said. "She really hates to be kept waiting."

I suppose Brian wasn't having the time of his life, either, because he didn't argue or try to drag the date out to the last minute. He just asked the waiter for the check and insisted on paying it, although I offered to pay half.

As we were standing up, the sound of loud laughter caused me to look over at a table near the door. There was Liza Shore, otherwise known as Big-Boned Beauty, sitting with a short guy with thick glasses. They were holding hands across the table and seemed to be having a lot of fun.

"Claudia!" Liza called, catching sight of me. I suppose this was another instance of my overnight fame, since Liza and I had never officially met.

"Hi," I said.

"Claudia, you should be proud of yourself," Liza said. "Nathan and I met through your column. He answered my ad and we've been having a great time together, haven't we, Nathan?"

"We sure have," Nathan agreed. "I knew I didn't meet Liza's height requirement but I'm fascinated by ancient Egypt and it's rare to find a girl who is, so I took a chance."

"Next week our parents have arranged to drive us to New York so we can see the Egyptian exhibit at the Metropolitan Museum," Liza said. "We've been at the library all morning looking up facts about the Egyptians so we'll be prepared. Did you know that many of the pharoahs were believed to be quite short?"

"Although some think Cleopatra herself was a big-boned beauty," added Nathan.

"Thanks, Claudia, for getting us together," Liza said.

"You're welcome," I replied. Even though they made a sort of goofy couple, it was great to see two people who hit it off so well — unlike Brian and me.

Brian brought me my jacket and we went outside. "They found each other through my column," I told him.

"That's nice," he replied.

We stood in front of the Rosebud Cafe and waited for my mother to arrive. Yeah, I thought to myself. It was nice. Lucky them.

CHAPTER 11

Julie Stern stood up from her slanted artist's desk and walked to me with a worried look on her face. Julie is the layout artist for the *Express*, which means she's responsible for taking all the material the printer sends back to her and making sure it fits into the paper in an attractive way. "It's still too long, Claudia," she said. "I can't fit all these ads into the space I have."

"Uh-oh," said Stacey who was sitting beside me at my desk, helping me sift through the ads.

"But I thought we had extra space this issue," I replied. This was the third installment of Claudia's Personals and the staff had voted to give me an extra half a page. I sure needed it in order to deal with the ton of ads I was getting. The kids sounded so eager to make contact with each other that I hated forcing them to wait several issues to see their ads.

But, that was just how it would have to be.

Julie laid the large white board she'd been working on across my desk. Each board was divided in two by a blue line and represented two pages of the newspaper. Julie was taking the typeset material she'd received from the printer and cutting it into columns the way it would look in the actual paper. "I've used every inch of the extra space we gave you," Julie insisted. "You're going to have to cut at least four ads. I need to lose about twenty lines."

"Four ads!" I cried. "I just can't. As it is, some of those letters have been sitting in my box since the very first issue."

"Sorry, Claudia," Julie said. "Maybe you can shorten each ad. That way you won't have to cut anyone completely out."

"We've already shortened them," I told her. Stacey and I had worked for hours to get each letter down to its most compact form before typing them up and handing them in.

"We'll have to shorten them again," Stacey said with a resigned sigh.

"The paper is supposed to go to bed tonight," Julie told us. "We don't have time to reprint anything. Can you make the cuts right now?"

"How?" I asked, confused.

"Cross out the lines you don't want, then

I'll cut them out with my X-Acto knife," she said, holding up what looked like a sharp metal pencil with a slanted razor blade at the end. I'd used an X-Acto knife once when I was working on a collage in art class. The knife is extremely sharp and made for very precise, delicate cutting.

"You know, maybe it would be easier if I did the cutting myself," I suggested. "That way I could take a little from here and a little from there instead of driving you crazy with every change."

Julie looked anxiously at the wall clock. It was already four. "Okay," she agreed. "I have so much other material to lay out, that that would help me a lot. Let me show you how." Julie gave us a quick course on cutting and pasting lines together with the knife and a clear glue which came in a metal can with a brush attached to the top.

Stacey and I set to work. We started by taking out single words at the ends of sentences that took up an entire line. (Emily had told me those were called *widows* in editorial talk.) Then, each ad kid lost one of their great characteristics. *Raven-tressed, history buff with romantic streak*, became *history buff with romantic streak*, as I carefully cut out the words *Raven-tressed*.

"It's okay with me if she loses her raven

tresses, but now we need a capital H for history," Stacey pointed out.

"We can cut this big H from Hang-tough Harry's name," I said. "But should we call him just Hang-tough or just Harry?"

"Cut out Hang-tough," said Stacey. "It's longer so we'll save more space that way." So, using the knife, I cut out the word Hang-tough and then gingerly cut out the capital H and brought it to where we needed the H for history buff.

"This isn't so hard," I said, proud of how quickly I was picking up the knack of cutting and pasting.

"It's a good thing you're an artist," Stacey commented as she watched over my shoulder. "Not everyone would have a steady enough hand to make those letters look straight. I don't think I would."

"No? To me, this is a snap," I said confidently.

Well, that's what I thought at first. But an hour later my eyes were crossing from peering down at all those little letters, and my fingers were sticking together from the glue I was using to piece everything in place. "I'm losing my mind," I complained to Stacey as I rubbed my eyes with the backs of my hands.

"Me, too," Stacey agreed with a yawn. "Maybe we could just take out this ad Mary

Anne put in for Logan. She's our friend. She'd understand."

"We can't. I promised her I'd run it." Bleary-eyed, I peered down at Mary Anne's ad. *Your cuddly kitten will love you furever. Call The Tig at 555-8456.* Mary Anne thought it would be fun to send Logan a secret love message through the column. She'd used the nickname Logan sometimes used for her, which was also the name of her cat, Tigger. "If I cut out the word *cuddly* I can move *Call The Tig at 555-8456* up a line and get rid of a whole line," I said, cutting as I spoke. I did the cutting and moved the words around. "I can do it with the ad above it, too," I realized, and cut that apart, as well.

I was just about to paste all my snipped words into place when I felt a hand on my shoulder. Startled, I jumped, sending the column onto the floor.

"Sorry," said Emily, kneeling to help me pick up the small pieces of paper which had scattered. "Are you done with that? The printer is here to pick up the mechanicals." (Mechanicals is more newspaper talk for the boards on which the printing is laid down.)

"I think so," I said, jamming the words back into position and quickly pasting them in place.

Emily looked over my work. "You did that

like a real pro, Claudia. It looks great."

"Claudia's a natural with anything connected to art," Stacey said.

"Would you ever be interested in doing layout work for the paper?" Emily asked me.

I smiled wearily. "Not as long as Claudia's Personals keeps me busy. I don't think I could handle anything else. But if you ever cancel the column, I could help with the layout."

"There's no way this column is getting canceled," said Emily taking the mechanical from me. "It's the hottest thing in the whole paper."

Emily went to the door to talk to the printer and I slumped down in my chair, feeling beat. "Well, we did it," said Stacey, stretching. "Let's get out of here."

"Good idea. But I'm too tired to move."

Stacey pulled me out of my chair. "Come on."

"All right," I said. "Let's go." Outside the school, a blast of cold winter air woke me up. But when I reached my house, I was tired all over again. My mind was swimming with little words and letters. If I shut my eyes I could almost see the letters floating around in front of me. I had to give Julie Stern a lot of credit. Laying out that newspaper was hard work.

The next morning when I arrived at school, Claudia's Personals was once again all anyone was talking about. Everyone had a copy of the

Express. "How do they print it up so fast?" I asked Emily when I saw her in the hall.

"They have a staff that works all night," Emily told me. "And they have this amazing, gigantic computerized photocopier that can print them up super fast once they have a master copy of each page. It does everything —print, put the pages together, even staple them. It's not as professional as a real news-paper or magazine, but I think it looks pretty good. By the way, at the next student council meeting, I'm going to ask for more money so we can print more issues each week. We used to need only a certain number of copies of the paper. Now, because of your column, every single kid wants a copy."

"Are you glad about that, or is it a big pain in the neck for you?" I asked.

"No! I'm really glad," said Emily. "Each year the school board has been chopping out more and more after-school activities so they can save money. If the paper is really popular it won't get cut. Your column is the best thing that could have happened to the *SMS Express.*"

"I'm glad, too, then," I said. Funny, I'd thought up this column to find Mr. Perfect. But, I was really starting to care about the paper, to feel like a part of it.

By lunchtime I was in a great mood. I was glad that I'd contributed something to the paper, I was enjoying being famous among the students, and I was momentarily *not* thinking about my failure to find Mr. Perfect. As I walked into the cafeteria, though, my good mood melted when I saw Mary Anne's puffy, tear-stained face.

"What's wrong?" I asked, slipping into a chair at the table where Mary Anne sat with Stacey and Kristy.

"Logan won't speak to Mary Anne all of a sudden," Kristy said.

"Why not?"

Mary Anne burst into tears. "I have absolutely no idea."

CHAPTER 12

On Friday, Stacey and I lay draped across my bed waiting for everyone else to arrive for the BSC meeting. We were feeling pretty down because of Mary Anne. "I hope she can survive this," I said as I turned a page of the *Express*. Stacey and I were flipping through it as we talked, not paying much attention to anything in it. "She's *so* upset."

"I'd be upset, too," said Stacey. "Logan won't even tell her why he's so mad. That would drive me crazy."

"Me, too," I agreed. "And it's not like Logan to act this way. What could possibly be wrong?"

"Beats me."

Stacey and I stopped talking and started thumbing through the paper. I hadn't even looked at my column since it came out (after all, I knew what was in it). I decided to see how my cut and paste work looked.

That's when I saw *it*.

"Oh, no," I said, feeling my cheeks go pale.

"What? What's wrong?"

"Look at Mary Anne's ad," I told her, feeling sick to my stomach.

Stacey's eyes opened wide as she looked down at her copy of the paper. "Oh, no. You pasted *Call the Tig* onto the ad above it."

The ad now said: *Fed up girl with dud boyfriend looking to make a switch. I'm pretty, petite, and sweet. Call The Tig at 555-8456.*

The ad below it said: *Your kitten will love you furever. Call Starting Fresh at 555-9302.*

"I want to die," I said, covering my face with my hands.

"It certainly explains why — " Stacey began. She cut herself off as Mary Anne entered the room. Mary Anne had dark circles under her eyes and looked as if she hadn't slept since Wednesday.

"What explains what?" she asked glumly as she plunked herself down on the end of the bed.

Stacey and I exchanged anxious glances. But before I could answer her, Mary Anne continued, "As if things aren't already weird enough, this afternoon I got a call from some boy wanting a date. He called me The Tig and everything. Logan is the only one who calls

110

me that. Do you think he could be telling guys to call me? Like . . . like . . . he wants to get rid of me for good." A tear trickled down Mary Anne's cheek.

"Mary Anne, I'm *sure* that's not it," Stacey said.

"How can you be sure?"

It was time for me to confess my mistake. "Check out your ad and the ad above it," I said, handing her the paper. "It was a mistake. Honest, Mary Anne. I only saw it myself a minute ago."

Mary Anne's brows knit in confusion as she read the ads. "How did this happen?" she asked.

I explained to her about the deadline rush and my quick cut and paste job. When I had finished, Mary Anne smiled — and then started to cry. "I can't believe I didn't see this," she said through her tears. "I've been so upset about Logan, I didn't even look at the paper."

"Don't cry, please," I pleaded. "I'm so sorry. I don't know what to say. I'm just so, so, so sorry."

"It's okay," Mary Anne replied. "I'm so relieved. But poor Logan. He must be so *hurt*. Why didn't he talk to me?"

"I guess he thought you were fed up with him," Stacey pointed out.

"Poor Logan," Mary Anne said again. "Now I'm going to have to write him a note and hope he reads it."

"Maybe he'll talk to me," I said. "I could explain everything to him."

"Would you?" Mary Anne asked.

"I think I owe you that much," I said, picking up the phone and dialing Logan's number.

When Logan heard my voice, he was immediately defensive. "If you've called about a baby-sitting job, fine. If you want to talk about Mary Anne, forget it."

"Wait! Don't hang up! This whole thing is my fault." I told him what had happened. "And if you don't believe me, check with Emily Bernstein or Julie Stern. They were there and they know I was cutting and pasting in a hurry. Emily might even remember how I dropped the mechanical board since she helped me pick it up."

At that moment, Mary Anne took the phone from my hand. "The one you should be talking to is *me*," she said. "I can't believe you thought I put that ad in the paper! I'm sorry your feelings were hurt, but you hurt my feelings, too. Why didn't you trust me enough to at least talk about it?"

Sensing Mary Anne needed some privacy, Stacey and I went into the hall. As we stepped out, we met Kristy charging up the stairs.

"You guys won't believe what I found in your column," she said excitedly.

"We know," I told her. "Mary Anne is in the room talking to Logan now. It was a paste-up accident."

"That was really dumb," said Kristy, at her tactless best.

"Thanks a lot," I said.

"Well, it *was* dumb. Though I'm sure you didn't mean to do it. I suppose stuff like that can happen pretty easily."

I took Kristy's copy of the *Express* and sat down on the hallway carpet. "I better read the rest of this thing. Who knows what other horrendous mistakes I might have made?"

I didn't see any other mistakes (thank goodness), but I did notice something that I hadn't realized before. Some of the kids seemed like perfect matches. It was right there in the paper. For example, one girl wrote: *I'd love to hear from someone who doesn't run with the crowd. I need a quiet person for talks, reading together, and long walks. Call Still Waters Run Deep at 555-2738.* Half a column down a boy wrote: *I get overlooked because I'm quiet and shy. But if you love walks, talks, poetry, and shared dreams, call Romantic but Shy at 555-4829.*

I mean, was that a match made in heaven, or what? Yet I wondered if they would see it or pass one another by. That would be such a shame. Then I got an idea. I could run an ad advising Still Waters to contact Romantic but Shy, or vice versa. Why not?

Mary Anne appeared in the doorway, still looking puffy but smiling.

"All patched up?" I asked hopefully.

Mary Anne nodded. "We still have some things to talk about but at least we're talking."

"Great," said Stacey.

Getting to my feet, I checked my watch. It was five-twenty. "I have just enough time before the meeting to call Starting Fresh and explain what happened," I said.

I called her number, expecting her to be roaring mad at me. Instead, she was thrilled. "I've gotten so many phone calls you wouldn't believe it," she told me happily. "I guess everyone is looking for a kitten to love them forever. And get this! One of the calls was from my boyfriend! He almost croaked when he realized I was the kitten."

"Gee, I'm sorry," I said, not quite knowing *what* to say.

"No, it was great! That means he wasn't happy with our relationship, either. He wanted to go out with another girl. It gave us a chance to talk about the reasons we aren't happy."

"And you patched things up?" I guessed.

"No, we broke up. But now I don't have to

feel like the bad guy. We can say it was mutual, which is better for everybody. Thanks, Claudia. You're a genius."

"I wouldn't exactly say that, but I'm glad things worked out," I said.

"They sure did. Keep up the good work."

"Thanks." I hung up the phone feeling much better. I wasn't a life wrecker, after all.

CHAPTER 13

"Claudia, I thought the personals column was just a cool accident, but now I think you must be some kind of genius," said Emily. We were standing in the *Express* office about two weeks after the Mary Anne-Logan-near-disaster. This was the second time in two weeks that I'd been called a *genius*. It seemed so weird. All my life Janine had been the genius. No one had *ever* called *me* that.

The reason Emily was so full of praise was because the paper had just come out with my first installment of Claudia Advises. It was instantly popular.

Here's how Claudia Advises came into existence. In the last issue, I had placed my ad advising Romantic but Shy to contact Still Waters. While I was writing up that ad, I remembered some other possible matches I'd seen in past issues. It occurred to me that No Wimp and Shy Beauty might get along since

116

they both loved nature. (No Wimp liked but-
terflies, at least.) I added them to my ad.

I also had a hunch that Rambling Rose might
do better than I had with Good Listener, since
he obviously wanted someone to carry the
conversational ball. (Since I'd never heard
from him again, I assumed he'd felt as awk-
ward as I had on our date.) Even though he
wasn't for me, Brian was a nice person. He
deserved someone nice (and someone who
wouldn't mind his lack of conversational
skills). From the sound of her ad, Rambling
Rose seemed to prefer a boy who didn't say
much. I added them to my ad, too.

After my ad came out, I was swamped with
requests by kids to match them up. Almost
every new ad came in with something like this
written on the bottom: *Claudia, if you notice
anyone who looks good for me, please let me know.*

In that issue, a new kind of ad started com-
ing in, too. They were thanks ads. *Big-Boned
Beauty says thanks a lot, Claudia. Me and little
Pharoah are in love.*

So, I started keeping a sharp eye out for
possible love matches. I found quite a few of
them. When Emily saw my love match ad for
this issue she commented that it was awfully
long, which was true. It took up nearly half a
column. "We should make it a separate article," I said as a joke.

At that, Emily smiled brightly. "Great idea! We'll call it Claudia Advises. All we have to do is add that title to what you've already written and draw a box around it."

"All right," I agreed, typing *Claudia Advises* on the computer above my ad.

It had seemed like a simple thing at the time, but if I had been thinking clearly I would have shouted: "No! No! Never!" I was taking on *more* work and a big responsibility. Maybe I had no business fixing people up. I mean, it was just my opinion. Yet, the thank-you ads kept rolling in, so I figured I must have some talent for matchmaking.

The only person I didn't have a knack for matching up was me! I hadn't found any ad that came close to meeting my requirements for the perfect guy. I'd even lowered my standards — well, slightly. I'd crossed "Easy to talk to (a good listener)" off my list. (I still wanted someone I could talk to, but after my last date I realized that I needed someone who could at least talk back. I had left "Interesting (lots to say)" on my list.)

The current issue wasn't any more promising, either. All the guys sounded geeky to me.

Finally, though, one afternoon after school I sat down to look through the ads for the next issue and one of them popped out at me. It said: *I'm getting desperate. I need a girl who doesn't giggle and act like a little kid and preferably one who doesn't wear pink. She should be smart, funny, pretty, and sort of hip. I've been told I'm good-looking, I play rock guitar, paint, and study eastern culture. No cheerleaders, please. Call Rock at 555-2984.*

He sounded pretty cool to me. Also, I fit his qualifications and I don't look good in pink. I decided to call him *and* place his ad, just to be fair.

I phoned him as soon as I got home. "Hi," I said, "Is Rock there?"

"Rock?" said a woman's puzzled voice. "Do you mean Richard?"

"I don't know," I confessed awkwardly. "Does he play guitar and like eastern culture?"

"Yes. Um, just a minute."

After a few minutes I heard a boy's voice. "This is Rock. Who's this?"

"Hi, I'm calling about your ad," I said, trying to place his voice and running through a mental list of boys from our class named Richard.

"I just put in my ad yesterday," he said suspiciously.

"Oh, well, I'm Claudia so I got the ad first," I explained.

"You're Claudia!" he cried. "Wow! Cool! Sorry to sound so dubious but I thought Alan was goofing on me."

Alarm bells went off in my head. "You don't mean Alan Gray do you?"

"Yeah, I do. I don't go to SMS. I go to a private school but I heard about your column and I gave Alan an ad to place for me."

"Are you a friend of Alan's?" I asked. If he was, he was out.

"That flake case? Nah. He's my neighbor. I've been stuck living next door to him since I was born. I must have done something in another life for which I got this horrendous punishment of being Alan's neighbor in this life."

That made me laugh, which was a good sign. "So, would you like to meet some time?" I said boldly.

"Absolutely," he agreed. "Alan told me that you were very cool. He wanted to date you himself. He was so bummed when you turned down his bogus ad. Which, in my estimation, vouches for your good taste."

"Alan is not my type at all," I said, tactfully understating the case.

"Want to go to a movie Friday night?" Richard asked.

"Sure, that might be fun," I said. I gave him my address and he said he'd come by and get me. "My older brother can drive us," he said.

I hung up just as Stacey came in for our Wednesday BSC meeting. "What's going on?" she asked. "Why are you grinning like that?"

"I just made a date with a guy who sounds super cool," I told her. "He says he goes to a private school. It must be the Paulson School."

"That's all boys, isn't it?" said Stacey.

"Yup. That would explain why such a great guy would have to place an ad in the paper."

"What's his name?"

"Rock, but it's really Richard."

"Rock?" Stacey laughed. "As in a large stone?"

"No," I said, laughing, too. "As in rock 'n' roll!"

When everyone else arrived, I told them about my new date. "He sounds weird to me," Kristy commented. "I don't see what was wrong with Brian Hall. If I didn't like Bart so much, I might go out with him."

"He would be more your type," I agreed. "But Rock sounds more like mine."

From that moment on, I thought of nothing but Rock: how I would create the cover for his first rock album; how he'd insist that I sing backup vocals onstage with him, although before that moment I'd never known I had singing talent. We'd ride around the countryside on his motorcycle (which I was sure he'd eventually get even though he was too young for one right now). We'd sit on a hillside and paint together. It would be so wonderful.

That Friday I couldn't wait for the BSC meeting to end so I could start getting ready for my date. At six o'clock I looked at my friends. They were all sitting around as if they had no intention of leaving. "Well?" I said. "Isn't anyone leaving?"

"No way," said Kristy. "We want to see this guy."

I crossed my arms. "Oh, no. I don't want some reviewing committee here to greet him. You guys are leaving. It's bad enough that my mother and father will give him the third degree."

"Let us just stay and see how you look on your date," said Mary Anne. "Come on."

"Oh, all right," I agreed. Truthfully, I was glad they stayed. It kept me from melting into a nervous puddle. "But what about supper?" I asked.

"We have a little money in the treasury," said Stacey. "We could probably afford to order in pizza."

I ran downstairs and asked Mom if it would be all right to order pizza. She and dad had been about to order in Chinese food, so I ran back upstairs and asked how that would be. Everyone agreed it would be fine. Mom and

Dad added three more plates of ribs and sesame chicken to their order and even paid the
entire bill.

By the time my friends had called home to
ask permission to stay for supper, the food
had been delivered. We sat together in the
kitchen and ate quickly. Then we hurried upstairs to my room.

"You're not going to wear those, are you?"
Kristy asked as I slipped into my new brown
suede cloth pants.

"Why not?" I asked. I thought they were
the best thing I owned.

"I don't know," said Kristy. "They just
don't seem right for a first date."

I was *not* about to take fashion advice from
Kristy, of all people. "I like them," I insisted,
zipping them up.

"I don't believe you're telling her what to
wear, Kristy." Mary Anne giggled.

"I know what you should wear. Those bead
earrings," said Stacey.

"They didn't make a big impression on
Brian," I reminded her.

"Well, this guy sounds different. And wear
lots of silver jewelry. Your bangles would be
perfect. And put your good silver hairclip in."

I trust Stacey's fashion sense, so I took her
advice. I finished the outfit with a simple yellow button down shirt and a brown and yellow

brocade vest. "Perfect!" Stacey announced. "All you need is a little lipstick and mascara."

By the time I was done, even Kristy admitted I looked nice. By then, it was seven-fifteen. Rock was coming at seven-thirty. "Everybody out," I told them.

"Oh, come on," Mary Anne pleaded. "We'll stay at the top of the stairs and just look down. He'll never know we're here."

"I'll know you're here," I said. "I'm already nervous enough."

"All right. We're out of here," said Kristy.

They left and I spent the next fifteen minutes fussing with my hair and makeup. (I took my hair down and added a hint of brown eye-shadow.) At seven-thirty sharp, the doorbell rang.

I bounded downstairs, determined to answer it before one of my parents did. "Hi," I said to Rock, who stood there in jeans and a bomber jacket. His hair was brown and on the longish side, sort of flopping into his eyes, which were big and brown, and he had a handsome face, with nice high cheekbones. He wasn't very tall, but he was taller than me.

In minutes, my parents were behind me, ready for the grand inspection. I could tell from my mother's tight smile that she wasn't altogether pleased with Rock. Neither was Dad. "You're to be home by ten-thirty," he told me sternly. Then he turned to Rock. "What's your last name?"

"Brompton," he said with just the slightest edge of annoyance in his voice. "My dad is Richard Brompton. He's in the book if you need to call my house for any reason."

"I'm sure that won't be necessary," replied my father, not smiling.

We couldn't get out of there fast enough for me. "Wow, man, Alan didn't tell me you were a Japanese chick," Rock said as we walked toward the beat-up Chevy idling at the curb.

"I really hate being called a chick," I said, trying not to sound angry.

"Oh, sorry, I know a lot of girls don't dig that," he said. "It's just an expression."

"Does it matter to you that I'm Japanese?" I asked.

"Well, yeah," he said. "It's great. I'm into everything oriental. Like *yin yang*, *tai chi*, sushi, you name it."

"I hate sushi," I told him.

"You do?" He gasped as he held open the car door so I could climb in the backseat. "You mean you don't eat teriyaki and stuff like that?"

"I like teriyaki but we don't eat it all the time."

In the front was a guy with a long ponytail. "This is Russ, my brother," Rock told me.

Russ just grunted and pulled away from the curb. All the way to the mall, Rock quizzed me about Japanese things, most of which I knew nothing about. "Could we please not talk about Japan anymore?" I asked as we pulled into the parking lot.

"Why not?" he asked. "You're not ashamed of being Japanese, are you?"

"No," I told him. "I'm proud of it. But what is your background?"

"Hungarian and Polish."

"Do you speak either of those languages?"

"No."

"Do you know lots about eastern European culture? Do you eat goulash and kielbasa sausage every night?"

"Of course not!"

"Well?" I said pointedly as I climbed out of the car.

"Okay, I get your point," he said. "Cool earrings, by the way."

That was more like it. "Thanks," I said. "I made these myself from a bead pattern I saw in a museum. It's an authentic Native American pattern."

"I knew it," said Rock. "You almost look a little Native American. But you know, I believe the first Americans were of eastern origin. If you look at them you can tell they're easterners."

He was off again. What he knew about theories of eastern migrations from northern Russia and China down through Alaska was very interesting. But the way he kept talking about everything Asian made me feel as if I were some representative of Japan instead of just me, Claudia.

That evening we watched a good movie about a guy who came back from the Civil War, only people start to suspect that even though he looks the same, he's not really the same guy who left, especially his wife who likes the new guy better than her old husband.

I guess finding Mr. Perfect was never easy, even back then. As we left the theater, I was determined to keep Rock off the subject of Asian cultures. "Your ad says you paint," I reminded him.

"Yeah," he said. "I did the design for this." He began rolling up his sleeve until he came to what he was looking for — a tattoo of a skull with roses growing out of it and worms crawling on top. It was gross! (Well done, but gross.)

"Is that a permanent one?" I asked.

"It's the real thing. It hurt like anything and I was grounded for a month because of it, but it was worth it," he said proudly. "I'll have this baby for the rest of my life."

"Do you think you'll want it when you're forty?"

"I can't imagine being that old," he said, rolling down his sleeve. "You know, body painting is something that's found in many ancient cultures."

"I suppose so."

"Want to get something to eat?"

"No, I don't think so. Can we call your brother to come get us? I'm kind of tired."

"Sure," said Rock, looking disappointed.

It wasn't long before Russ's jalopy came banging and sputtering into the parking lot. When we finally pulled up to my house, Rock took my hand. "Can I kiss you good night?"

"I don't think so," I said, pulling away. "Good night. It was nice meeting you." I practically ran up the front steps and into my house.

Of course, my parents were sitting up in the living room. "How did it go?" asked my mother.

"He was fine, just a little bit odd," I said.

"Odd in what way?" Dad asked.

"He was very polite," I assured him. "We just didn't get along."

"All right. You're home early."

"I was tired," I said. I kissed them both and then went upstairs to my room. From under my bed I took out my list of qualifications for the perfect guy. Then I picked up the phone and punched in Stacey's number.

"Home already?" she asked.

"It was a bomb. The only thing the guy could talk about was Asian things. He had a totally one-tracked mind."

"Was he interesting, at least?"

"I suppose so."

"That was one of your requirements," Stacey reminded me.

"Yeah, but he was a little too interesting. He had a skull tattoo."

"Ew," said Stacey. "I see what you mean."

After hanging up with Stacey I looked over my list. Was I being too particular? Maybe. I crossed *interesting* off my list. But then I made an addition. *No tattoos.*

CHAPTER 14

Tuesday

Yesterday was a first. My first dog swearing in ceremony. Claudia and I presided over Pow's transition from Barrett dog to Pike family pet. It was Claud's brilliant idea.

I think it helped the kids. But I wunder if Pow new what was hapening.

On Tuesday, Mrs. Pike got a call to do some secretarial work for a company in Stamford. I went to the Pikes' to help out Mallory for the afternoon. Mal is allowed to sit for her brothers and sisters as long as another sitter is there (the usual Pike rule) and she doesn't exhaust herself.

When I arrived, the Pike kids were wild with excitement. The day before, the workers had finished putting up the high wooden fence around their backyard. Now they were ready to take ownership of Pow.

"I really should be here for this," Mrs. Pike fretted as she pulled on her coat. "But if I push this event back one more day I think the kids will go nuts. Do you girls think you can handle it?"

"No problem," I assured her. "Everything is under control."

"There may be tears," Mrs. Pike warned. "Buddy and Suzi, I mean."

"Oh, I hope not," said Mal.

"We can deal with it," I said.

Half an hour after Mrs. Pike left, Mrs. Barrett arrived with Buddy, Suzi, and Pow on his leash. "He's here!" cried Margo, dashing to the front door. "He's finally here."

The kids came pouring in from every corner of the house. They swooped down on Pow, hugging him, petting him, and dancing around him happily.

Poor Buddy and Suzi. Buddy clutched a brown paper bag and looked as if he were choking back tears. Suzi, her bottom lip puffed out, clung to her mother's hand. "What's in the bag?" I asked Buddy.

"Dog stuff," he said, handing it to me. Inside were a red bowl, a half-opened bag of dry dog food, three cans of wet dog food, an old blue squeeze toy in the shape of a bone, and a slightly chewed rawhide knot.

"He won't have to sleep outside, will he?" Suzi asked Claire.

"No, we bought him a bed. It's plaid," Claire told her.

"Well, kids, say good-bye to Pow and let's go," said Mrs. Barrett.

"Can't we stay with him?" Buddy pleaded.

"We don't want to leave him," Suzi insisted.

Mrs. Barrett looked at me.

"It's okay by me," I told her.

"Me, too," said Mal.

Mrs. Barrett left, but Buddy and Suzi hovered in the doorway. They looked lost and unhappy.

"I think this important moment deserves an important ceremony," I said.

Mal picked up on my idea right away. She ran to the closet and pulled out a red plaid dog bed. "Pow should sit here, as if it's his official spot," she said.

The kids liked the idea and gently prodded Pow onto the bed, and he settled in. Then the kids looked to Mal and me.

"I think the Barretts should say *au revoir* to Pow," I suggested.

"What's 'o-river'?" asked Suzi.

"It's the French way to say good-bye," I explained. "It doesn't mean good-bye forever. It means, until we meet again." (I'd learned that late one night while watching an old movie about World War Two.)

"Until we meet again," Suzi repeated, a slow smile spreading across her face. "That's good."

"Yeah," Buddy agreed.

"Who wants to start?" Mal asked.

"I will," Suzi volunteered. She stood in front of Pow, her back straight and her head held high. "O-river, Pow," she said with a hint of drama. "You've been a good dog. Try not to hate Marnie for making you leave. She's just a dumb baby. She didn't know her allergy would make you leave. Behave yourself. Don't chew up Claire's slippers like you did my troll slippers last week when I sneaked you into the house. Don't drink from the toilet, and I promise to come see you soon." Suzi kissed Pow on his head and then stepped back.

Buddy took his cue and stepped forward. "Or-revor, Pow," he said solemnly. "We'll meet again. Don't you worry. All your favorite stuff is here and the Pikes are nice people so I know they'll treat you nicely. I'll come see you." He knelt to hug Pow. "See ya soon."

"Do the Pikes want to say anything?" I asked.

Jordan Pike stepped forward. "I would like to welcome Pow to our house," he said. "We are very, very glad to finally have a dog so we'll be the best dog owners a dog could ever wish for."

Adam tapped Jordan on the shoulder then and whispered something in his ear. "Okay," Jordan whispered back. "Plus we wish Buddy and Suzi to know that they have full visiting rights."

"I hope they're better than the visiting rights my father has with us," said Buddy, looking worried.

"You can come see Pow any hour of the day or night, any time, ever," said Jordan.

"Any time?" Buddy repeated.

"Call first if it's after midnight," Mal told him, smiling. "But, otherwise, just come right over."

"All right!" Buddy cried. Suzi looked as if she felt a lot better, too.

"Is there more to the ceremony?" Jordan asked Mal and me.

"There's a large package of Oreos on top of the refrigerator," Mal said. "I think we should celebrate now." Mal ripped open the package and proclaimed, "Here's to Pow, one of the few shared dogs in the history of dog ownership." Then she handed out the cookies. The kids touched their Oreos together, saying, "Here's to Pow!"

"Do you want to see some tricks Pow can do?" Suzi asked the Pike kids.

Of course they did, so the kids moved back into the living room where Pow demonstrated his ability to roll over, play dead, and bark exactly three times on command.

"Is he a good watch dog?" Byron Pike wanted to know.

"Well, he likes to watch *Scooby-Doo* on TV," Buddy told them, which sent everyone into a fit of laughter.

At about five-thirty, Mrs. Barrett called and said she was coming by for the kids. "Franklin and I are taking them out for pizza and a movie to cheer them up," she told me.

"They're doing pretty well," I told her. "I don't think you have to worry."

But when the time came for them to part from Pow, it wasn't quite as easy as I'd hoped.

Suzi started crying, and Buddy's nose grew red from holding in his tears. "We'll take really good care of him," Vanessa Pike told the kids. "You don't have to worry about anything."

"Okay," said Buddy, pressing his lips together. "Or-revor, Pow."

"Come on, kids," Mrs. Barrett urged gently. "Let's go."

They waved to Pow one last time, then turned to leave with their mother. Pow barked and scrambled to the door, ready to leave with them.

Mallory caught Pow by the collar and held him back. "You're staying here, Pow," she said softly. "This is your home now."

CHAPTER 15

By the time I had suffered through a third bomb of a date, I was completely disgusted. I'd answered an ad placed by a boy named Kurt. Like Brian and Rock, he'd sounded great on paper, but the reality hadn't been even close to my Mr. Perfect. Kurt was okay — for someone else. But to me, he was *boring*!

That Friday night after my date, as I glumly dragged myself up the stairs (we had gone to a movie, and then Kurt spent another hour at a video game arcade), I decided it was time to take the situation in hand. I was going to place my own ad in my own column.

I flopped on my bed and then hung upside down to find my Mexican-print stationery under the bed. That's where I'd stashed my perfect guy list. With that in hand, it would be easy to write my ad.

I put my list beside me, then reached across to my desk and grabbed my spiral notebook.

Maybe it was because I was becoming desperate, but the words seemed to flow pretty easily that night. Here's what I wrote: *Eigth-grade girl how loves art, misteries, and lafter seeks boy who is handsum with some musles, medium height or taller, atheletic, sensative, artistic, a good dreser, not too criticil, has no tattos, and can make me lagh. Write Chosey but Fair at.* . . . I included my address but not my phone number. I didn't want to be put on the spot over the phone. I wanted time to go over the responses to my ad and pick just the right ones.

I decided to put the ad into the next issue and not think about it anymore. But, as the weekend wore on, I found myself changing my ad just a little here and there. I changed the beginning to *Pretty eighth grade girl with long black hair*, and I took the muscles off my list since I thought that sounded shallow. If the guy was handsome, that was good enough.

I'm not sure what did the trick, but not long after my ad came out the responses started *pouring* in. Luckily I would arrive home from school before my parents arrived home from work, so I could gather up all the letters addressed to Choosey but Fair. (I'm not sure they would have loved the fact that I was advertising for a boyfriend. They might have thought it was undignified.) Each afternoon I ran upstairs with my letters and tore them open.

Honestly, I don't know why some of them even bothered to write. One boy said: *I'm a guy who loves sports, especially football. I don't know much about art, but you can teach me. (Ha! Ha!) I love girls with long black hair. Do you look like Paula Abdul? I hope so.*

What a jerk!

The other letters weren't much better. It was pretty disappointing.

One afternoon I was in the *Express* office sorting through more ads when I pulled out a letter addressed to me. I recognized the handwriting, but I couldn't remember why. I opened the letter and this is what it said: *Dear Claudia, Please don't print this. I'm writing to thank you for sending me to Dr. Reese. She's really cool and understands what I'm going through. She's helped me realize that my parents' divorce isn't my fault and that they both still love me. Thanks for taking the time to care. Yours, Sean.*

"I don't believe it! You're actually reading something and smiling." Stacey had come into the office as I was holding the letter. "Don't tell me. It's another ad that looks perfect to you."

"No," I said with a laugh.

I handed her the letter. "Oh, that's so nice," she said. "That's even better than finding Mr. Perfect."

"I've practically given up on *that*." I made

a disgusted face. "It makes me feel like a fraud. I mean, here I am fixing up all these couples and — "

"Oh, by the way," Stacey interrupted me. "I just saw Brian Hall walking down the hall with Rose Marie Montey. They looked very cozy."

"Motormouth Montey?" I laughed. "She's *got* to be Rambling Rose. She doesn't stop talking for two minutes. She and Brian will be perfect. He'll never have to say a thing!"

"Another success," said Stacey.

"But what about a success for me?" I demanded. "Why can't I find someone for myself?"

"Maybe your standards are a little . . . I don't know . . . too high," Stacey suggested delicately.

I plunked my chin onto my hands. "I'm not going to settle for someone I don't really like," I told her. "But it's pretty discouraging. I put my ad out there saying exactly what I wanted and not even one guy was able to write a decent ad. They are all so obviously not Mr. Perfect that it's scary."

"Well, maybe Mr. Perfect hasn't seen your ad yet," said Stacey. "Why don't you place it again in this issue?"

"I guess I will. Though I don't think it will

do much good. The letters have started to dwindle down in the last few days. I think I've gotten all the responses I'm going to get."

Stacey shrugged. "You never know."

I didn't have much hope, but I ran the ad again anyway. Two days went by and nothing came in for me. Then, on the third day I found a letter in my mailbox addressed to Choosey but Fair.

Dear Choosey, it said. *I'm an eighth grade boy at SMS. I love track, going to art museums, reading mysteries, and great works of literature. I'm five-foot eight, haven't got a single tattoo, and I've been told that I look like Jason Priestly. I don't see how I could ever be critical of someone who sounds as lovely as you. Your Guy.*

My heart started to beat faster as I read the letter a second, and then a third time. I snatched up my list and looked at my requirements. If he looked like Jason Priestly, that was handsome enough for me. If he ran track he probably had just the right kind of muscles I was looking for. (And he wasn't making that up to impress me, since I'd crossed muscles off my list.) He was definitely taller than me. We had mysteries in common and if he liked great literature that meant that he was probably both sensitive and interesting. He loved art museums, which was artistic enough. (I said I was fair. He didn't have to be Picasso to be artistic.) And, best of all, he thought I sounded lovely. That fulfilled my last two important requirements — he wasn't critical and he was crazy about me.

He *was* Mr. Perfect. Mr. Right. My dream guy.

I just had to read his letter again. But my heart skipped a beat as I realized something about his letter. There was no real name, no phone number, and no address on it!

Was my Mr. Right being mysterious? Or was he just plain stupid? No, not this guy! He was definitely not stupid. Maybe another letter was coming. Maybe he just wanted to build up the suspense before showing up on my doorstep with a dozen roses.

The next day I couldn't think of anything but finding *him*. In the hall I smashed into my history teacher because I was so busy gawking at the boys who passed by, searching for a Jason Priestly lookalike. I saw one guy who had the Jason Priestly look. I ran to him, but then slowed down. He was shorter than me. "Sorry," I apologized. "I thought you were someone else."

At lunch, I barely ate a bite. I didn't want to miss *him* while I looked down to cut my turkey plate special. "What if he thinks he

142

looks like Jason Priestly but he really doesn't?" Kristy wondered. (I'd told my friends about Mr. Right.)

"This guy wouldn't lie," I insisted. "He sounds too down to earth."

"If I were you, I'd narrow my search to the track team," Mary Anne suggested. "Maybe Logan knows who you're talking about."

"Great idea," I said. "Too bad it's not track season. I could watch a practice if it was."

Kristy shook her head skeptically. "There are no Jason Priestlys on *our* track team, I can tell you that."

"You wouldn't know," I said. "The only guy you pay any attention to is Bart."

Kristy shrugged. "Well, I never noticed anyone who looks like Jason Priestly. That's for sure."

"I don't see why you have to find him," said Stacey. "If it's meant to be, he'll find you eventually."

"No way. I've waited long enough. I'm not waiting any longer." I threw my napkin on top of the gluey gravy covering my turkey and got up.

"Where are you going?" Mary Anne asked.

"I'm using the rest of my lunch break to find him. First I'm going to the boy's gym to get a list of guys on the track team. Then I'm going to the library to try to find out if any guys have checked out art books or mysteries. And don't wait for me when school's over," I told them. "I'm going to stand at the front door and check out every guy who passes. If that doesn't work, I'll be at the side door tomorrow morning."

"Gee," said Mary Anne. "You're some detective."

"I haven't been reading all those Nancy Drew books for nothing," I said with a smile. I was determined to find my dream guy.

Just when I thought I was about to collapse from my exhausting (and unsuccessful) search for Mr. Right — he showed up. Well, to be exact, another letter from him showed up in my mailbox. It said: *Hi, Choosey. It's me again. I just wanted to tell you that I will show up — someday. Right now I might seem mysterious, but believe me when we meet you'll know it. Until then, you can be sure that I am Your Guy.*

Again, no name, no address. I was ready to tear my hair out.

I went to my room and called Stacey. "I can't stand it another second," I told her. "He wrote again but he didn't tell me how to find him."

"Well, maybe he just wants you to know he's out there," said Stacey.

"What good does that do me?" I cried. "Knowing he's there but I can't find him is far, *far* worse than not finding the perfect boy."

"It is?" Stacey asked in a strange voice. "Then I'd better come over right away."

Why? I wondered. I guess I'd really worried her. I must have sounded as if I were going crazy or something. I *was* going crazy! She was right.

Ten minutes later, Stacey appeared in my room. "That was fast," I said.

"Claudia, I have something to tell you."

"What?" I asked, alarmed.

"I wrote those letters."

"What letters?"

"Mr. Right's letters." She cringed, waiting for me to explode.

Which I did.

"What?" I yelled. "Why? Why would you do such a terrible thing?" I was *so* disappointed — and hurt, and furious, and confused. "Was this your idea of a joke?"

"No, no," Stacey said, taking a few steps toward me. "I thought you might feel better if you knew the perfect guy at least existed."

"How could you think that?" I demanded angrily.

"I thought it would be like with Pow. Buddy

and Suzi feel better knowing he's out there, knowing he's at the Pikes', if not at their house."

"Well, I wasn't looking for a dog! I was looking for a person!"

"I know it's not the same," Stacey said, her voice full of apology. "Once I saw that Your Guy was torturing you, I wrote the second letter hoping to make things better. But when you called I could tell I'd just made everything worse. So that's why I'm here—to set things straight. I'm really sorry, Claud. Please forgive me."

"I can't," I said, turning away from her. "I think you better go." I stood with my back turned until I heard Stacey's footsteps on the stairs.

Then I sat on my bed and dissolved in tears. I don't know which was worse, the trick Stacey had played, or knowing that Mr. Perfect really wasn't out there.

The next day, I went back and forth between being angry and sad. When I saw Stacey, I'd feel angry. Maybe she hadn't meant to hurt me, but she had. Best friends should know one another better than to do something so completely stupid.

Then I'd feel sad as I watched the guys go by and realized there was no longer any sense in looking for Mr. Right. He simply wasn't there.

I stayed mad through Tuesday, but by the BSC meeting on Wednesday, I was starting to soften. After all, Stacey had meant well. And I couldn't look at her puppy-dog eyes and please-forgive-me expression much longer without caving in.

It was Kristy, though, who (in her own bossy way) patched things up. "What is going on between you two?" she demanded to know shortly after the meeting started.

"Claudia is mad because I did a really dumb thing," Stacey spoke up. "I don't blame her for being mad," she added.

"What did you do?" Shannon asked.

Stacey told her story. "Oh, no!" Jessi cried. "Do you mean Claudia was looking for a guy who didn't exist?"

"Exactly," I said. Somehow hearing the story out loud made it seem more funny than tragic. "Pretty dopey of me, wasn't it?" I said, starting to laugh.

My laughter opened a floodgate of laughter. "It wasn't dopey. You didn't know," Mary Anne said loyally between giggles.

"I'm sure you'll find somebody nice some day," Shannon said reassuringly.

"Do you know what?" I told her. "I'm giving up my search for him. If he does exist, he and I will probably find one another when the time is right."

"That's all I was trying to say to you," Stacey said cautiously.

"I know," I said, reaching over and hugging her. She hugged me back. It was good to be friends again.

The phone rang. Mrs. Barrett was looking for a sitter. "She says whoever takes the job will have to walk Buddy and Suzi to the Pikes' to visit Pow," said Kristy, who had taken the call. "They visit him every single day."

"That's great," said Shannon.

"The baby-sitter who goes will also have to feed the gerbils, make sure the hermit crabs don't escape, and feed the fish," Kristy went on. "The Barretts are accumulating non-allergic animals fast."

"Good for them," said Stacey. "I'm glad they're adaptable."

Adaptable — flexible. Able to change depending on what was happening. Was I being adaptable? Or was I sticking too rigidly to my made-up idea of the perfect guy? When I found him, would he be anything like I'd imagined?

I gave myself credit for being at least a bit adaptable. I'd started a column to find Mr. Right. Instead, I'd discovered a new talent (as well as the wonders of Spellcheck). I could run a column, give advice, and actually help people. This was an important discovery.

I also discovered that finding Mr. Perfect wasn't so important after all. I had my friends. And I had myself. Everything I needed to be happy had been right here all along.

About the Author

ANN M. MARTIN did *a lot* of baby-sitting when she was growing up in Princeton, New Jersey. She is a former editor of books for children, and was graduated from Smith College.

Ms. Martin lives in New York City with her cats, Mouse and Rosie. She likes ice cream and *I Love Lucy*; and she hates to cook.

Ann Martin's Apple Paperbacks include *Yours Turly, Shirley; Ten Kids, No Pets; With You and Without You; Bummer Summer;* and all the other books in the Baby-sitters Club series.

THE BABY-SITTERS CLUB

Look for BSC #72

DAWN AND THE WE ♥ KIDS CLUB

Bleeeep! The phone chirped as Sunny was explaining to Jill about waxing surfboards.

Sunny grabbed the receiver from her night table. "We Love Kids Club," she said. "Hi, Mr. Robertson. . . . Yes, we're all here. . . . A week from Saturday? Hang on."

(All this point in a BSC meeting, Claudia would tell the parent she'd call right back. Then she'd hang up while Mary Anne was carefully looking through the record book, checking every possible scheduling conflict and trying to make sure each was getting a roughly equal amount of work.)

Not the We ♥ Kids Club. "Dawn, are you busy that day?" Sunny asked with her hand over the mouthpiece.

"I don't think so," I replied.

"Okay, Mr. Robertson, Dawn'll be there," Sunny said into the phone. " 'Bye."

End of conversation. No muss, no fuss.

Eventually Sunny put her board away and we turned to our other favorite topic — food. The W♥KC has a health-food cookbook, and each of us keeps a file of personal recipes that we update all the time.

Maggie was in the middle of describing a scrumptious soba noodle dish, with sesame paste and watercress, when the phone rang again.

"We Love Kids Club!" Sunny announced into the phone. "What? Who *is* this?

Sunny's brow got more and more wrinkled. "Uh-huh . . . okay . . . I guess . . . um, can I call you right back?" She rummaged in her night table drawer, took out a pencil and a piece of paper, and scribbled a number. "Got it. 'Bye."

We were staring at her as she hung up. "What was that about?" I asked.

Sunny looked dumbfounded. "She says she's a feature-story writer from the *Palo City Post* — Ms. Lieb."

"What did she want?" Jill asked.

"She said she's writing a series of articles about kids who runs businesses. She heard about the We Love Kids Club and wants to make an appointment to interview us!"

THE BABY-SITTERS CLUB®

Hello, fans!

Although it's wintertime, it's never too early to think ahead to spring and this season Scholastic and I have come up with a special challenge just for you. We want all Baby-sitters Club fans to **GET INVOLVED!** Here's the challenge:

1. Think about an issue that matters to you and your community. It might be recycling or volunteering at a local hospital or shelter, or it might be something completely different! How would you get involved and help? Think about how the members of the Baby-sitters Club get involved, like Jessi when she works with the Kids Can Do Anything Club in JESSI'S WISH (#48). You can make a difference, too!

2. Write me a letter which describes, in 50 words or less, how you propose to **GET INVOLVED!** Tell me what's important to you about your selected cause and how you plan to take action.

3. Send in your letter. My assistants and I will be reading all the letters and selecting the ones which make an impact—letters we feel suggest the best and most creative ways to help others. More details about the prizes are included on the entry form.

I'm looking forward to hearing from you. When I was younger I was a candystriper at a local hospital and I later helped at a summer camp for handicapped children. Now that I'm older, I have a foundation which helps children and the homeless, and another foundation that creates children's libraries for kids who don't have easy access to books.

Even the smallest contribution matters—and getting involved can be an exciting adventure for you and your friends! So get set and **GET INVOLVED!**

Happy Writing!

Ann M Martin

WINTER CHALLENGE!

If you're a BSC fan, you know that the Baby-sitters are always active and busy in their community...and not just with baby-sitting. When Stoney-brook needs help, the girls are ready to pitch in. If you're concerned about the town you live in, write a one-page letter about 50 words telling us your plan for improving it.

ENTER AND YOU CAN WIN:

GRAND PRIZE

• A $10,000 US Scholarship Savings Bond sponsored by Milton Bradley®, makers of The Baby-sitters Club Board Game and The Baby-sitters Club Mystery Game, and Kenner Products, makers of The Baby-sitters Club Dolls.

2 FIRST PRIZES

• A book dedicated to you, your cause and your community.
• A visit from Ann Martin to your hometown and local bookstore for an autographing and lunch.
• Plus..loads of quality BSC merchandise and a **BSC GET INVOLVED** sweatshirt, signed by Ann Martin.

100 RUNNERS-UP:
Win a **BSC GET INVOLVED** sweatshirt.

Just fill in the coupon below or write the information on a 3" x 5" piece of paper and mail with your **"GET INVOLVED"** letter to the appropriate address. U.S. Residents send entries to: **SCHOLASTIC INC., BSC WINTER CHALLENGE**, P.O. Box 742, Cooper Station, NY 10276. Canadian residents send entries to Iris Ferguson, Scholastic Inc., 123 Newkirk Road, Richmond Hill, Ontario, Canada LAC 3G5.

Rules: Entries must be postmarked by March 31, 1994. Winners will be judged by Scholastic Inc., and Ann M. Martin and notified by mail. No purchase necessary. Valid in the U.S. and Canada. Void where prohibited. Employees of Scholastic Inc., its agencies, affiliates, subsidiaries, and their immediate families are not eligible. For a complete list of winners, send a self-addressed stamped envelope after March 31, 1994. to: THE BSC WINTER CHALLENGE Winners List, at either address provided above.

- -

Attach this coupon to your **GET INVOLVED!** Letter.
THE BABY-SITTERS CLUB WINTER CHALLENGE

Name _____ Birthdate _____

Address _____ Phone# _____

City _____ State/Zip _____

Where did you buy this book? ❑ Bookstore ❑ Other (Specify) _____

Name of Bookstore _____

HAVE YOU JOINED THE BSC FAN CLUB YET! See back of this book for details.

BSC993

by Ann M. Martin

More titles... ▶

The Baby-sitters Club titles continued...

❑ MG45658-X	#57 Dawn Saves the Planet	$3.50
❑ MG45659-8	#58 Stacey's Choice	$3.50
❑ MG45660-1	#59 Mallory Hates Boys (and Gym)	$3.50
❑ MG45662-8	#60 Mary Anne's Makeover	$3.50
❑ MG45663-6	#61 Jessi's and the Awful Secret	$3.50
❑ MG45664-4	#62 Kristy and the Worst Kid Ever	$3.50
❑ MG45665-2	#63 Claudia's ~~Freind~~ Friend	$3.50
❑ MG45666-0	#64 Dawn's Family Feud	$3.50
❑ MG45667-9	#65 Stacey's Big Crush	$3.50
❑ MG47004-3	#66 Maid Mary Anne	$3.50
❑ MG47005-1	#67 Dawn's Big Move	$3.50
❑ MG47006-X	#68 Jessi and the Bad Baby-Sitter	$3.50
❑ MG47007-8	#69 Get Well Soon, Mallory!	$3.50
❑ MG47008-6	#70 Stacey and the Cheerleaders	$3.50
❑ MG47009-4	#71 Claudia and the Perfect Boy	$3.50
❑ MG47010-8	#72 Dawn and the We Love Kids Club	$3.50
❑ MG45575-3	Logan's Story Special Edition Readers' Request	$3.25
❑ MG44240-6	Baby-sitters on Board! Super Special #1	$3.95
❑ MG44239-2	Baby-sitters' Summer Vacation Super Special #2	$3.95
❑ MG43973-1	Baby-sitters' Winter Vacation Super Special #3	$3.95
❑ MG42493-9	Baby-sitters' Island Adventure Super Special #4	$3.95
❑ MG43575-2	California Girls! Super Special #5	$3.95
❑ MG43576-0	New York, New York! Super Special #6	$3.95
❑ MG44963-X	Snowbound Super Special #7	$3.95
❑ MG44962-X	Baby-sitters at Shadow Lake Super Special #8	$3.95
❑ MG45661-X	Starring the Baby-sitters Club Super Special #9	$3.95
❑ MG45674-1	Sea City, Here We Come! Super Special #10	$3.95

Available wherever you buy books...or use this order form.

Scholastic Inc., P.O. Box 7502, 2931 E. McCarty Street, Jefferson City, MO 65102

Please send me the books I have checked above. I am enclosing $—————
(please add $2.00 to cover shipping and handling). Send check or money order - no
cash or C.O.D.s please.

Name _____ Birthdate_____

Address _____

City_____ State/Zip _____

Please allow four to six weeks for delivery. Offer good in the U.S. only. Sorry, mail orders are not
available to residents of Canada. Prices subject to change.

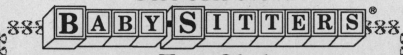